Other Series by Harper Lin

The Patisserie Mysteries

The Emma Wild Holiday Mysteries

The Wonder Cats Mysteries

The Emma Wild Mysteries

www.HarperLin.com

Sweets and a Stabbing

A Pink Cupcake Mystery Book 1

Harper Lin

ISBN-13: 978-1987859355
ISBN-10: 1987859359

Contents

Chapter One

Amelia Harley stood in front of the pink truck, her eyes wide, arms folded across her chest, with tears dangerously close to spilling over her bottom lids.

"You did it, Mom," her daughter Meg said. "You really did it."

"Yeah." Amelia hugged the girl close to her. "You like the name? The design? You think it looks okay? You don't think a pink truck is too much?"

"The Pink Cupcake? I love the name!" Meg walked up to the hulking food truck and ran her hand across the smooth letters. "And it has to be a pink truck so no one will get you confused with Burrito Loco or Charming Wok's. Plus, all my friends won't be able to miss it. That will be good for business."

"Yes, hungry teenagers would be good for business." Letting out a deep breath, Amelia nodded in agreement.

The Pink Cupcake might not have looked like much to anyone else. It was a hot-pink rectangle on wheels. Opening the large windows on the left side would reveal the inside of the truck, where Amelia would not just sell her sinfully delicious cupcakes but also bake the little morsels in three ovens throughout the morning and noon rush hours. Dainty little jars held her confectioner's sugar, flour, cocoa, and dozens of other ingredients.

After jumping through half a dozen bureaucratic hoops, she had finally gotten her vendor's permit and reserved her spot on the Food Truck Mile, which was snuggled between the financial district and the shopping district of Gary, Oregon. Lots of foot traffic. Lots of tourists. Lots of business. That's what Amelia was hoping for.

"Where is your brother?" she asked. "I thought he'd want to see the truck, too."

Meg rolled her eyes as she usually did when she spoke about her older brother, Adam. "Where he always is. In his cave, avoiding sunlight for fear he'll disintegrate."

"Stop. Your brother is more introverted. Like me. You are the extrovert, like your father." That comment rang with more truth than Amelia was willing to share with her daughter at the moment. She had made a conscious choice not to say anything bad about her ex-husband within earshot of the kids, no matter what.

"You aren't an introvert, Mom. At least, you aren't any more. Not if you're going to be in business for yourself." Megan pulled her long brown hair over her right shoulder, twisting it around her fingers.

"I'm nervous," Amelia whispered.

"What for? You're your own boss now."

* * *

If anyone would have told Amelia she'd be managing her own food truck, she would have laughed in their faces. A year before, she'd had a husband to take care of, a four-bedroom house to manage, two kids to love, shopping to do, social events to attend, and lots of Joneses to keep up with. Today, she was renting a two-bedroom house with a basement and detached garage.

What a difference a day can make. It was a beautiful afternoon in Gary, Oregon, when her world completely shifted. Like those homes in the Ozarks that are built on tender, delicate stilts to avoid flooding, Amelia's life had become a balancing act, and her job was to keep everyone happy. One pleasure she allowed herself was to lunch with The Girls once or twice a month. Those were the only opportunities Amelia got to be a woman. She wasn't mom or wife or even Mrs. O'Malley. She was just Amelia. During one of those lunches, the last lunch she attended, to be exact, the floodwaters rose too high to ignore.

"Who does your landscaping?" Amelia asked her closest friend, Christine Mills, while they were at Gatto's Restaurant with the rest of the girls. "I'm just about ready to give up on those rose bushes I have–tear the whole thing out. I've got loads of thorny branches and no flowers."

"We use Gary Custom Cuts, but they aren't really great." Christine rolled her eyes. "They're good enough to mow the grass, but I wouldn't trust them with much more than that."

"Why?"

Only after Amelia heard Christine's unfortunate experience with Gary Custom Cuts Landscaping cutting down her wild-flower garden did both women realize they were the only ones talking.

"What's wrong with you guys?" Amelia asked while her eyes bounced from Denise to Linda to Sarah then back to Denise again.

Nervously, the three women glanced back and forth among each other as if waiting for permission to speak.

In hindsight, that display was what had hurt Amelia the most.

Chapter Two

Those three women, who asserted they were Amelia's friends, knew her husband was having an affair. How long they'd held on to that information Amelia couldn't be sure. But she found it very suspicious that they never told Christine, who would have marched over to Amelia's house the minute the rumor started and told her about it.

"We only just found out about it," Denise insisted as Linda and Sarah nodded in agreement.

"Did you know about this?" Amelia turned to Christine, who sat there in shock, scowling at The Girls' behavior.

"No" was all she said as she shook her head, looking suspiciously across the table.

Of course Christine hadn't known. The girls hadn't told her. They held on to the juicy bit of gossip, feeding it and nurturing it like a poisonous weed, just waiting for the chance to spring it on Amelia before her husband got up the courage to tell her himself.

That would have happened in private. Mr. O'Malley would have never confessed his infidelity at Gatto's Restaurant, causing the scene of Amelia blubbering and stammering away like someone suffering from Tourette syndrome.

To add insult to injury, Sarah made sure that Amelia knew the other woman was only twenty-five years old.

"What could a girl that age possibly have to offer?" Sarah asked, as if her comment couldn't be answered by any man over the age of fifty, as John O'Malley was.

That fact twisted in Amelia's gut. If only her husband hadn't made it so obvious that he wanted someone prettier. She almost thought she could've accepted it if the other woman had a PhD or was the wealthy widow of an oil tycoon. But she was just hot. That was all.

The girls seemed to know a lot about the other woman, but Amelia stopped listening. Instead, her mind screamed that she couldn't help aging. Unlike Denise, Linda, and Sarah, she refused to get any kind of "work" done. Botox and boob jobs on a Thursday afternoon didn't sound like fun. Besides, she wasn't unhappy with her looks. For a forty-four-year-old woman, her figure had blossomed into a lovely hourglass. She might not ever make the cover of *Sports Illustrated*, but that never mattered to her.

"We're so sorry, Amelia." Linda reached across the table to try to take Amelia's hand, which she pulled away quickly.

"Yeah, if there is anything we can do, just let us know," Sarah added, nodding and again looking at Denise and Linda for their gaze of approval.

"You didn't have any idea?" Denise asked.

There it was. The question to inflict more pain and watch her squirm.

Christine took her other hand, lying limply in her lap, and pulled her up from the table like a little girl struggling to stay awake past her bedtime.

"We're leaving," Christine hissed.

Without putting up any kind of fight, Amelia stood, squared her shoulders, and bit the inside of her cheek to keep the tears from falling. She squeezed Christine's hand as if holding on were somehow keeping her on the ground or above water or any other euphemism for not dying of humiliation right there on the spot.

The Girls sat there without moving, as if they had looked at the face of Medusa and become frozen in stone.

* * *

Snapping back into the present, Amelia stroked her daughter's hair and suggested they go into the house to celebrate with some ice cream and an old movie before bed.

"*Sunset Boulevard.* Please! Please!" Meg said.

"We've seen that a thousand times." Amelia smiled.

"Yes, and it just keeps getting better."

Telling Meg no was difficult. She managed straight As in school and had a small side job helping Mrs. Logan next door with keeping up her yard and dogsitting her two rambunctious pugs, Sugar and Spice.

"Alright, *Sunset Boulevard* it is."

* * *

After the movie, both she and Meg went to bed, but Amelia didn't sleep. She crept downstairs to the basement, which her sixteen-year-old boy, Adam, had claimed for himself. He was also asleep, sprawled across his bed with his mouth hanging open and his laptop resting dangerously close to the edge of the mattress.

She tiptoed up to him, took the computer, folded it, and set it on the floor. Amelia thought he looked just like his father. That wasn't a bad thing. John O'Malley was a handsome man, and Amelia couldn't say otherwise. She wished she could say that, after they split up, he gained a lot of weight, lost his hair, and developed a scorching case of eczema on his neck and hands, but he didn't. He joined a gym and got buff, and his hair refused to leave his scalp. When he came to pick up the kids for his scheduled visits, he was always wearing some clingy polo shirt or trendy T-shirt with the Batman logo or something equally juvenile on it.

But Adam didn't have his father's personality. He was quiet. He liked what he liked and didn't care what people thought. He was his own person, and that he was like that at the age of sixteen assured Amelia she was somehow doing something right.

She made her way back upstairs, poured herself a small glass of wine, and sat up in her bed sipping it, thinking of nothing and everything all at once, feeling like a kid starting at a new school in the morning.

In her mind, Amelia had a vision of herself floating gracefully from oven to oven to the cash register to playfully chitchat with the customers and her fellow vendors. She fell asleep to her own voice saying, "It's going to be fine. It's going to be just fine."

Chapter Three

The next morning, Amelia was up before the sun. After getting dressed, she went outside to double-check the contents of the truck, her mind ticking every last minute detail off her list. The gas tank was full. All her permits were properly displayed in the window. The fire extinguisher was securely fastened to the left of the ovens. She had stopped at the bank the day before and gotten plenty of change.

By the time she had finished, Meg and Adam were up, dressed, fed, and walking to the bus stop.

"Good luck!" Meg squealed, standing on tippy-toes to kiss her mom on her cheek.

"Thanks, honey."

"Good luck, Mom," Adam said as he was walking away, a little too cool to give Mom a kiss in front of the other kids, who were already stationed at the corner, waiting on the same bus—especially Amy Leonard, who carried a skateboard as Adam did.

Amelia waved and took a deep breath. She waited a few minutes then watched her kids climb aboard the big yellow bus. Finally, when they were out of sight, she burst into tears.

It was just first-day jitters causing all the waterworks. How many times had she burst into tears since this big plan had taken root in her mind? A million at least. She cried when she got the permit. She cried when she got her ovens installed. She cried while she baked her first set of cupcakes in them. She cried after she hired Lila, her only employee. Now, she was crying because it was do-or-die time.

Wiping the tears away, she revved the engine and pulled out of the driveway.

"That's it." She sniffled to herself, wiping her nose on her sleeve. "No more crying for you, Amelia. Not until Meg gets married. From now on, nothing will shake you up."

She looked at the sky, which had started off as a glorious sunrise of pinks and yellows, only to transform into a dreary gray mat. A few droplets splattered on the windshield.

"A quick shower. No big deal. This is Oregon, after all. Quick showers happen all the time." She soothed herself as she drove the truck out of the driveway. "You're acting like you didn't grow up here, like you are some noob from one of those weird rainless states like Arizona or Nevada." She flipped on her windshield wipers.

By the time she snuggled her truck into her designated slot on Food Truck Alley, the sprinkles had turned into a downpour. The only person outside was a lunatic in pink rubber galoshes and a yellow raincoat and hat stomping and kicking through the rain puddles. That was Lila Bergman, Amelia's only employee. She waved and headed over.

"Hey, you made it! Don't worry." She climbed up the back of the truck, took off her raincoat, and stuffed it into a small cubby underneath the fire extinguisher. "You're supposed to have a crappy first day at a new job. If it starts off great, it can only go downhill. Start off like this, the only way to go is up." She smiled widely, flashing the gap between her two front teeth.

Amelia had to laugh. There was something about Lila that Amelia really liked. Maybe it was that she was divorced, too. Or perhaps it was that she was such a free spirit, not above running barefoot in the rain or skinny-dipping at midnight or wearing a tiara and a feather boa while grocery shopping.

But during their interview, what Amelia had liked the most was Lila's brutal honesty.

"I guess you could say I was a secretary for the past several years," Lila confessed, as if being an administrative assistant was something to be ashamed of. "I've had about twelve secretarial jobs in the past five years. I got fired from them all."

The red flags started to go off in Amelia's head. Did she want to take a chance on a middle-aged woman who couldn't hold a job?

"I know what you're thinking. Then why hire me, right? Someone with a work history like that? Well, you certainly don't have to. The truth is that I am not cut out to be a secretary. I can't sit in a cubicle all day, and I can't wear pantyhose."

Amelia sat motionless at the small table for two at Café Lee, where she had decided to conduct her interviews. "Is that all?"

"Isn't that enough? Have you ever worked in an office, Miss Harley?"

Amelia had never worked anywhere. Of course, she'd worked in her own home, but that was work she enjoyed, with the exception of pulling weeds. She absolutely hated yard work.

"It's depressing. Let me tell you, a secretary has no hope of ever being anything else. I didn't want to grow old filing papers, staring at a computer, making reports I don't understand for people who saw me as replaceable." Lila let out a sigh but kept her back straight. "I am divorced with no children. My ex-husband has up and moved to Australia, and I'll never see him again, thank heavens. I have a knack for numbers. I'm honest to a flaw. Your books will be immaculate, and I'll monitor the supplies as if we were implementing wartime rations. That is the best I can do." She flashed her gap-toothed smile. "Plus"—she lifted her red-polished fingernail, pointing toward the sky—"if things get slow, it's not above me to break into my own version of Tom Jones's song 'It's Not Unusual.'"

Amelia started to laugh. "Why does that suddenly make me want to have a slow first couple of days?"

They spoke a few times after the interview. Amelia offered her the job, apologizing for the low wage, but promised a good deal of freedom, and as the business grew, so would the hourly rate.

Only later did Amelia find out that Lila didn't need a job of any kind. She was probably one of the wealthiest women in Gary, Oregon. But that was a story for another time.

The rain fell harder outside. The women chitchatted as Amelia gave Lila a tour of where everything was. She turned on the ovens and got her ingredients ready for the day. They were already measured and needed only to be mixed together. She thought that would be the most efficient way to bake in such a small space.

A few lessons were learned in the first hour at Food Truck Alley.

Lesson one: don't wear flip-flops. Amelia nearly killed herself half a dozen times by slipping on the metal grated floor where a few sprinklings of flour had fallen.

Lesson two: the three ovens didn't all cook at the same temperature. The batch of lemon-poppyseed cupcakes came out slightly underdone and dented just slightly under the weight of the ginger glaze spread over the top. The red-velvet cupcakes in the second oven had a smokier flavor because they burned just enough to make them food for the birds in the park across the street. Thankfully, the third oven was right on par for the double-chocolate cupcakes with a raspberry-chocolate frosting Amelia had concocted herself. Meg called it her signature cupcake.

Lesson three, and the most annoying: the chalkboard listing the day's creations was wiped clean by the rain.

Amelia had thought it a good idea so she could easily change things up each day. She realized she would have to come up with another way to list the specials of the day. Magnets? Painted boards?

As she wondered, the rain slowed down.

Amelia's thoughts were interrupted when Lila tapped her on the shoulder and pointed at the truck next to theirs. "Have you met our neighbors yet?"

Chapter Four

The truck to Amelia's right was the Turkey Club. They served huge, Henry VIII turkey drumsticks that made the area around their truck smell like Thanksgiving. To the right of the Turkey Club was the Burrito Wagon.

As Amelia strained her neck to look past the Turkey Club to the Burrito Wagon, she saw a very large man wearing cowboy boots that came to fine points that curved slightly upward. Tattoos were common in Oregon, but that man's seemed a bit overwhelming, as they covered his arms and crept up his neck, almost all the way up his bald head.

"Yikes. No one's going to complain about the food over there," Lila mumbled. "That's the kind of neighbor to make friends with."

Just as Amelia was about to look away, a small lady in a dress and Nikes came around to the front of the Burrito Wagon and patted the large man on the back.

"Hey, I know that lady." Amelia straightened up.

She grabbed one of her raspberry-chocolate cupcakes that was large enough for two people, slipped it into a hot-pink paper boat with a piece of wax paper over the top, and headed over to the Burrito Wagon.

"Mrs. Vega!" Amelia called as she tried to balance her cupcake while maneuvering around an ocean-sized rain puddle.

The old woman turned around. Smiling broadly, she waved. "Señora Harley! Hola."

"Hi." Amelia panted, a little out of breath. "It looks like we're neighbors at home and at work." Proudly, Amelia pointed to her big pink truck.

"Ay, that's your truck? It's beautiful!"

"Yeah. And here, this is for you." She handed her the cupcake. "To help your morning coffee go down."

"Oh, you're so sweet. Gracias. Thank you." She looked at the big brute adjusting the awning over the window. "This is my nephew, Matthew Rodriguez."

He turned around and gave a quick smile as he reached out a plump, beefy hand that engulfed Amelia's completely.

"Hello," he said quickly and went back to fixing the awning.

Amelia wanted to stare to try to figure out what the elaborate, scrolling letters said on his neck but found her manners, nodded in response, and looked back at Mrs. Vega.

"You come by after closing and take home meal tonight for you and the kids. Two burrito feed you guys for three days." Mrs. Vega let out a laugh as she patted her nephew on the back.

"I'll do that. Thanks, Mrs. Vega. Nice to meet you, Matthew."

* * *

Once back safely out of the elements and inside the Pink Cupcake, Amelia and Lila played a game of cards and waited for the rain to end.

"You're not very good at Go Fish," Lila teased. "I didn't think there was anyone who could be bad at Go Fish."

Amelia laughed and shook her head.

"I'm sorry. My mind is just going over the numbers in my head. I know what I need to make each day to break even. Any day that I don't make that, I'll have to try for double the next day. It's just... frustrating."

"Don't worry. It's too early to panic." Lila looked out the open window and inhaled deeply. "This rain won't last."

She was right. After another hour, the rain stopped as quickly as it had started. Like bees to honey, the lunchtime crowd scurried out of their buildings wearing galoshes, carrying umbrellas, and looking for sustenance.

The rest of the day flew by as Amelia baked more of the special cupcakes of the day while Lila handled the cash. No matter how busy she got, Amelia made sure each of her creations had the special little touches that she thought set her apart from other bakers, like a fresh raspberry on the top of her raspberry-chocolate cupcakes, with a pinch of powdered sugar for contrast. The lemon-poppyseed cupcakes were decorated with three little silver balls of candy in the center of each, with half a purple bachelor button flower that could also be eaten. They were little works of art that tasted heavenly.

By the time Mrs. Vega dropped off three giant burritos—she didn't want to leave Lila to go hungry—Amelia's tiny kitchen looked as if a tornado had hit it. Lila calculated the receipts while Amelia cleaned and secured everything for the drive home. After everything was done according to code, Lila gave Amelia the news.

"Here's the damage for the day." She handed Amelia the total and watched.

A smile spread across her face. "This is correct?"

"I'd bet my life on it."

"This means we made a profit of fourteen dollars and thirty-seven cents."

Lila grinned.

Amelia wanted to cry but remembered her promise to herself from that morning. Swallowing hard, she let out a giggle, tucked the receipt in the bag to turn in to the bank, and hugged Lila tightly. "Thank you. If you hadn't been so optimistic, I might have just turned around and gone home this morning."

"If I weren't optimistic, I wouldn't have taken this job at all."

Declining a lift home, Lila hopped off the truck and walked in the direction Amelia had seen her come from that morning. She stepped outside the truck to wind down the awning, and a familiar voice startled her from behind.

"Hey!" It was Adam.

"Hey," Amelia said, smiling. "Where is your sister?"

"She got a ride home with Katherine and her mom."

"You didn't want to take a ride with the BFFs?"

Adam rolled his eyes and snorted. "I have something for you," he said, handing his mother his cell phone.

"What's this? You're giving up your phone? You're going to learn how to read books with pages and catch fireflies after the rain and—"

"Mom."

"Oh, sorry. I thought that's what you were doing. Okay, tell me what I'm looking at." She smiled, watching her boy smirk. That was the best smile she could get out of him, and she was happy for that.

"I set you up with a webpage, blog, Facebook profile, Twitter, and Instagram accounts and have a trademark pending for the Pink Cupcake."

Amelia watched as Adam scrolled through the pages, everything bursting with the hot-pink color to match her truck.

"It's beautiful, honey. But how am I going to keep on top of this? I barely know how to turn on your laptop." She smiled.

"See, that's the beauty. These are all linked, so if you update one, it will automatically update the rest. All you have to do is post a thought or a special or a recipe or coupon, and it will transfer to all the other outlets. I doubt even the Kardashians are as immersed in the Matrix as you are now."

Pulling her son close, she kissed him on the forehead. That required she stand on tiptoe. "This is really great. Thank you. Hey, I've got burritos for supper from–"

"You shut up! You think I'm scared of you?" A man's voice was coming from the direction of the Burrito Wagon.

Amelia couldn't understand the muffled reply, but then another explosion of words made them both jump.

"This isn't over! I'll be back! Yeah! Come down here and say that to me!"

Carefully Amelia stretched and looked around the Turkey Club to see what was happening. Adam moved to look too, but Amelia held him close, not wanting him to get too close.

A man was stomping off down the sidewalk, his arms flying and his voice rising and falling while he continued to carry on the argument he'd had with whoever was at the Burrito Wagon.

"I know that guy," Adam said. "That's Mr. Indesh. Peter Indesh."

"Ruth Indesh's husband?"

"Yeah."

"Didn't he used to be partners with Bill Banks at your skateboard shop?" Amelia asked.

"Shooshies. Yeah. Used to. Until he started stealing money. I'm going to go see who he was yelling at."

"You'll do no such thing." She held Adam by the back of his shirt collar. "Respect people's privacy and their right to argue when they want. It doesn't concern us."

"But aren't you curious?"

"Too many cooks spoil the broth." *And the marriage.* "The Vegas are our neighbors down the street at home. We don't want to act like greedy hogs, sniffing around in their business. They can handle whatever it is, I'm sure." Amelia didn't mention the size of Mrs. Vega's nephew but was sure she was as safe as a kitten whenever he was around.

Adam rolled his eyes and slumped.

"Need a lift home?"

"No. Swooshies is getting some new Port Nation gear I wanted to check out."

"Okay. Be home right after," Amelia said. "We've got mutant burritos for dinner, and if you're too late, your little sister will eat a whole one herself."

"All right, Mom."

Her son hopped on his skateboard and headed toward his favorite home away from home.

Finally, she climbed into the cab of her truck—the front seat feeling like a mound of down pillows—revved the engine, and pulled out of Food Truck Alley. She hadn't realized it, but that was the first chance she'd gotten to sit down all day. Her legs and back cried with relief. It was the kind of exhaustion that came with knowing you did your best.

Amelia yawned as she stopped at the bank to make her deposit. Before heading home, she also made a stop at the St. Michael's Food Pantry to donate two dozen cupcakes that hadn't been scooped up by the end of the day. Nothing had gotten really burned. There had been no accidents. No one came running back to the truck clutching their stomachs claiming ptomaine poisoning. Plus, she had fourteen dollars and thirty-seven cents in the till. This was a fantastic day.

* * *

The following days were an absolute landslide of business. The weather was great, with the majority of rain peeking in between mostly sunny skies. The customers were lining up, requesting dozens to take to their offices and asking if the Pink Cupcake did weddings or bridal showers. Amelia found it all very encouraging.

"Weddings and showers. That's not a bad idea." Lila's eyes widened.

"No. It certainly is not. But I think we better get this truck under control first and then see how we can branch out."

"Yes, proceed with caution, of course, but cupcakes at a bridal shower is as logical a partnership as peanut butter and jelly."

"Oh, now there's an idea. Peanut-butter-and-jelly cupcakes." Amelia began composing a list of ingredients in her head in order to try the new concoction and bake a couple of test batches at home. "Can you believe it's Friday already?"

"Nope," Lila said while wiping down the counter. "This sure does beat the heck out of working in some office." She leaned out the window to take in the scenery and see what, if anything, was going on.

"Don't fall out," Amelia teased.

Lila pulled her head back in and smiled. "Have you met the people at the Turkey Club?"

Amelia shook her head. "No. I've seen the woman who runs it and waved hello a couple times."

"Did she wave back?"

"Yeah. I think she is a workaholic, you know. No time for socializing. Just do the

J-O-B. Nothing wrong with that." Amelia shrugged.

Lila nodded. "What about the guy on the left? What does he sell? Philly cheesesteaks?"

"Yeah." Amelia said, looking down at the decorating project she was working on. If she wasn't careful, her frosting would end up looking like slugs rather than delicate orange petals.

"That's it? Yeah?"

Amelia felt a blush fall over her cheeks.

"Wait a minute. What? Are you... blushing?"

Amelia said nothing but shook her head.

"Oh, I have got to go get a look at this!" Lila teased, dashing toward the back door.

"No, you will not. You are my employee, and you have to stay in the truck."

Lila froze, turned, and, flashing that gaping smile, waved her red-nailed hands toward herself. "Spill it."

"I haven't spoken to him." Amelia rolled her right shoulder up to her ear. "I just waved. Besides, hadn't you noticed that his customers are almost seventy-five percent female? Young females."

"No, but I will now," Lila said. "How old is he?"

"Actually, he looks like he's about our age. His hair is almost all gray, but it's cut really short, you know. Like he might have been in the service or something. He's no kid. But you don't mix business with pleasure."

"Certainly not. That would be just horrible." Lila laughed.

Suddenly a sharp, high-pitched scream echoed through Food Truck Alley.

Chapter Five

The words "He's dead!" rang out in a screechy, hysterical voice, and a collective gasp could be heard all the way from the picnic tables and benches, where the patrons would sit to eat when the weather was nice. This area was barely thirty feet from the Pink Cupcake.

The Dining Area, as the locals called it, was a beautiful section of the park shaded by dozens of large trees, bordered with various blooming shrubs and bushes that changed colors as the seasons did, and accented with flowers of every size and color. The benches lined the bushes, and from the vantage point of the Pink Cupcake, a mass of people had congregated by one of those benches facing away from them.

"Watch the truck," Amelia told Lila, who nodded her head and watched as some people dialed their cell phones while others clasped their hands over their mouths, their eyes bulging from their sockets as they looked at something gruesome in the bushes.

Amelia ran over and, pushing her way through the gawkers, finally caught a glimpse of the man. She too gasped. Without saying a word to anyone, she made her way back to the truck, climbed aboard, and took a seat, looking pale.

"What is it?" Lila patted Amelia's hand.

"It's a dead guy, all right. And I know him."

"What?"

"Yeah. He was just here, having an argument with someone from the Burrito Wagon."

"You're kidding."

Amelia shook her head. "His name is Peter Indesh. Or at least, it was his name. His wife Ruth used to work for one of the jewelers on State Street down in the shopping district, but she quit, wow, about two years ago. She was a really pretty girl. Long black hair. Weighed as much as steam."

"How long had they been married?"

"I'm not sure."

"Any kids?" Lila asked.

"No, and I say thank goodness because of this."

Lila nodded.

Within minutes, the sound of sirens approached quickly. The squad cars pulled up in front of Amelia's truck, blocking her in, as well as the Turkey Club, the Burrito Wagon, and the Philly cheesesteak guy. None of them would be going anywhere until the cops finished doing what they had to.

It was a long afternoon.

* * *

Finally, the police finished interviewing everyone who'd been in the vicinity of the dead body. Amelia eavesdropped as much as she could. Peter Indesh had been lying there for more than forty-eight hours. His wallet and keys were still on him. Cause of death: multiple stab wounds to the chest and neck. That was the clean version of what had happened. The autopsy would reveal that Peter Indesh's skull had been partially cracked by a blunt object. The stab wounds were made with a jagged-edged knife that sliced into his chest and his shoulders, as well as his throat, almost to the point of decapitation, and both of his eyes had been stabbed as well. A profiler would confirm that when someone had that kind of rage, the assailant was either on psychoactive drugs, in which case the body would be left where it fell, or the victim was the object of unrequited love.

She was sure it was nothing, but Amelia felt compelled to tell the officers of the altercation she'd seen on Monday night.

"Mr. Indesh was yelling at someone by the Burrito Wagon. I'm not sure if it was someone in the wagon or if it was another person just walking along."

"Could you tell what he was yelling about?" asked the detective, who had a very long name starting with a W and ending with a y.

"No. But Indesh was mad. He shouted all the way down the street until he disappeared around the corner. That was the last I saw of him until, well, today." She pointed toward the shrubs where the body had been found.

The detective gave Amelia his business card. She studied his name and was sure it had every letter of the alphabet somewhere in it.

"If you think of anything else, anything at all, just give me a call." He didn't smile back at her when she nodded and said she would.

Finally driving home, Amelia worried about Lila, who'd insisted on walking.

"My home is six blocks away," the woman had said. "The doorman knows me, and I'll be in his view as soon as I round the corner."

Walking to her apartment in the financial district where the doorman knew her, Lila Bergman was just as much a mystery as the murder was. However, Lila didn't make the ten o'clock news as Peter did. It was the headline, and when it popped up on the television screen in her living room, Amelia quickly snapped it off when Meg came in.

"Hey, honey. You getting ready for bed?" Amelia asked as Meg made her way to the refrigerator.

"Yeah. So when were you going to tell us about the murder in Food Truck Alley?"

Chapter Six

"Well, never, if I could help it," Amelia said. "You want to tell me how you found out about it? It only just came on the news."

"Internet, Mom." Meg rolled her eyes. "Plus, Katherine just texted me and told me all about it. She said she could see your truck in the background of the crime scene."

"Oh, brother."

"Don't worry, Mom. It isn't like you killed him."

Just then, a flurry of footsteps pounded up the basement steps.

"Hey, Mom!" Adam burst into the kitchen to find both Amelia and his sister already there. "Did you see the news? Peter Indesh? Dead right by your food truck!"

"Yes, honey, I was there when they found him."

"What?" Adam snapped. "You knew this happened and—"

"She didn't tell us," Meg stated matter-of-factly, putting one hand on a hip. "She thinks we're kids."

"Your interest in this ghoulish development is a little concerning to me." Amelia huffed as she went to get some water from the tap.

"Well, don't worry. I've got it up on your website, and—"

"You've what?" Amelia whirled around to face Adam. "You take that off of there right now."

"But Mom, all publicity is good publicity."

"Adam, if you don't take that down immediately, you won't be uploading anything until you graduate from college. I mean it. Whatever you have up there, take it down now!"

Her son let out a typical teenage sigh and rolled his eyes.

"Adam, Mr. Indesh was a neighbor of ours. He was someone's husband and someone's son. You need to remember that."

Nodding his head, Adam made circles on the linoleum floor with his foot.

"In fact, Ruth Indesh waved to us all the time when we drove past her house. I'm going to make her a casserole and dessert. Anyone want to help?"

"Yeah, sure. But let me fix your website first." Adam sulked.

"Thank you, honey." She looked at her daughter. "What about you?"

"I didn't think of it that way, Mom. I'm sorry." Meg's eyes brimmed with tears.

"Of course you didn't, honey. You're fifteen years old. You shouldn't have to. But since today changed that, that is what I'm here for. To help you figure it all out. Okay?"

Meg nodded and smiled.

"What should we make for Mrs. Indesh?"

"Maybe something that goes in the Crock-Pot. That way, it can be done in the morning, and we can walk it over to her first thing."

"Good call."

With just a few ingredients, Amelia, Meg, and finally Adam chipped in and made spaghetti and meatballs that cooked through the night and were just right by five in the morning, when Amelia got up. She had pulled a homemade pound cake from the freezer the night before. It was thawed and ready to be eaten, too.

On her way to Food Truck Alley, Amelia stopped at the Indesh residence and saw Ruth Indesh sitting alone on the porch, sipping coffee. She waved to Amelia as she made her way up the sidewalk.

"Hi, Ruth." Amelia couldn't hide the concern in her voice. "I was afraid I might wake you if I came calling this early."

"Hi, Amelia." She raised her cup as if proposing a toast. "Nope. I'm up. Been up in this swing all night."

Amelia nodded as if she understood, but she had no clue. She'd lost her husband the old-fashioned way, to a younger woman. She couldn't imagine how Ruth must be feeling.

"The kids and I thought you might not feel like cooking. We are so sorry for your loss."

"That was really thoughtful of you. Please tell Meg and Adam I said thank you. Truthfully, I'm okay with this. Yeah, I am. A man has to pay his debts. Somehow. Plus, divorce is so messy. No disrespect, but it is, isn't it?" She looked at Amelia with red-rimmed eyes. There was an unsettling calm there.

What did she just say? "I-I suppose?" Amelia said, still holding the Crock-Pot and the pound cake in her hands.

"I don't like messes. Peter made everything a mess. I guess there are lots of people who don't like messes."

Most people would just chalk this incident up to a new widow getting over the shock of being a new widow. But as Amelia watched Ruth set her coffee cup on the porch railing and push herself up out of the porch swing, she saw something else. Was it relief? Confidence? Sadness? Insanity? Amelia didn't know, but it made her uneasy nonetheless.

"I love spaghetti and meatballs. Please tell me these are real meatballs, too. Not some healthy turkey balls or tofu." She reached her hands out as she descended the white wooden steps.

"Nope." Amelia slowly shook her head. "Made with real beef and veal. And a pound cake for dessert. Made with real butter." As she handed everything over, she could see Ruth's hands were shaking.

"Again, please tell the kids I said thank you so much." Slowly, she turned, not waiting for Amelia to reply. "Oh, and I saw your truck on the news," Ruth said over her shoulder as she climbed back up to the porch. "You couldn't miss it. That's such a great color." With a few slow steps, she went inside her house and shut the door.

"What in the world?" Amelia muttered to herself, alone on the sidewalk. "She's got to be in shock. That's all. Everyone deals with grief differently, and she's just not sure how to act."

Trying to talk sense into a nonsensical situation, Amelia talked it out to herself as she drove to Food Truck Alley. She could have stayed home on Saturday, but since the little incident of murder had caused business to slump, she thought she'd put in half a day at least. There were quite a few other vendors who had the same idea. Turkey Club was in her usual space, as was Mr. Philly Cheesesteak and the Vegas' Burrito Wagon.

"Okay, so Ruth was acting strange. Who could blame her, right? I mean, if it were me..." She took a deep breath. "I'm probably not a good comparison. But it isn't like she said she was glad it happened. She just said she was okay with it. There is a difference. I think."

Opening the awning and sliding the window open, Amelia was not prepared to find a man standing right outside her truck and let out a loud yelp.

Chapter Seven

"John! What the...? You scared the bejeezus out of me."

"Hi, Amelia." Her ex-husband gave an awkward wave. The collar of his tight-fitting polo was pulled up around his neck. "The kids said I'd find you here."

"I'm sorry." Amelia shook her head. "Were you supposed to have them this weekend? I could have sworn this was a weekend at home, but with everything that's been going on, I could have screwed up."

"No. No. I'm not supposed to have the kids. I actually wanted to talk to you."

"Yeah? Well, if you don't mind doing it while I get set up." Amelia was sure this wasn't the talk that included the words *love, remarriage, or baby.*

"I saw your truck on the news last night."

"Isn't that something? I just dropped off a Crock-Pot of food at Ruth's house that the kids made for her. Such a shame." Amelia casually left out the weird exchange she'd had with Ruth, knowing John would've gone off on one of his pseudointellectual tirades about the grieving process, about walking a mile in someone else's shoes and the ultimate fear of death. Her stomach just flipped over on itself at the thought of it.

"I don't want you doing this," he said.

Amelia stopped wiping down the counter and stood up straight. "You don't want me doing what?"

"This, Amelia." He waved his hands in both directions, indicating the truck. "I don't want you doing this."

"If you're afraid of lightning striking twice, I don't think that is an issue. The police said whoever killed Peter knew him, and it wouldn't be long—"

"You're not hearing me, Amelia."

"I guess not." She pursed her eyebrows together.

John rubbed his hands together, licked his lips, and took a deep breath. "I am not looking forward to the questions people are going to have for me in the office Monday when they've all seen my wife's *food truck* was ten feet from a murder."

"That's *ex-wife*."

Jon clenched his teeth, making his jaw bulge. "Do you have any idea how this makes me look?"

Amelia couldn't be sure if a second, ten seconds, or a minute passed before she burst out laughing. "You're not worried about me." She chortled. "You're worried about you." She wrapped her hands around her middle and laughed hard. "Well, it's nice to see you haven't changed, John."

"This isn't funny. I'm important at work. I know that's hard for you to understand. It always has been. But I'm being groomed to take over the patients of Dr. Kumi. He has politicians, celebrities, real players as patients, and this just doesn't look right."

Amelia didn't know whether to laugh or cry out in anger.

"But it does look right to leave your wife of sixteen years and two children for a twenty-five-year-old. They like that where you work?" Her blood was boiling and her body beginning to shake. If the conversation wasn't brought to an end quickly, Amelia was afraid she'd make a scene.

"If it's about moncy, I'll request the court increase child support another, say, two hundred dollars." John huffed.

That was it. Amelia didn't care if she did make a scene. She turned, jumped off the back of the truck, and strutted up to John. Looking up at least six inches to his face, she pointed her finger at him.

"This has nothing to do with money, John," she hissed. "In fact, it has nothing to do with you at all. You think you can come to my business and tell me to shut it down because it isn't as pretty as your new life is?"

"You're getting this all wrong."

"No, I'm afraid you are. You lost the privilege to tell me what to do the day you stepped outside our marriage. I didn't do this to you, John. You did it. And if you ever come to my business again, trying to push me around, I'll have the cops here within seconds and tell them you're harassing me. How do you think that would look where you work?"

John hung his head. "I've got the kids next weekend. I'll be there at one o'clock. Have them ready." Turning on his heel, he thrust his hands into his pockets and stomped off.

Amelia let out her breath and climbed back into the safety of her truck. She did feel safe there, safe enough to cry without anyone seeing her. But she didn't cry. A promise was a promise. Instead, she swallowed hard, grabbed herself a bottle of ice-cold water, and took a long, deep drink.

She looked at the clock and gasped.

"Great. Thanks, jerk! Now, I have to rush."

The ovens were ice cold. The frostings weren't mixed. She wanted to make special sticky gingerbread cupcakes that had a list of ingredients as long as her arm. She'd never be ready in time. Instead, she opted for marbled chocolate cupcakes that took no time at all. That was one of the first recipes she'd perfected in her home kitchen and could conjure up from memory.

With notes taped to each oven, labeling which burned hot and which burned cold, she was able to get three dozen piping-hot batches out on display as the first customers arrived. Within minutes, John had already faded out of her mind, and only when she was locking up the truck and driving into the bank's drive-through with the receipt bag did she even remember he'd stopped by.

"Jerk," she mumbled, shaking her head.

* * *

Sunday really was Amelia's day of rest. Sleeping in until nine o'clock was like sleeping half the day away.

"Here, Mom." Meg said, bringing in a steaming-hot cup of coffee. "Has there been any news about the murder?" she asked, wiggling her fingers as a witch might over a bubbling cauldron.

"Not that I know of. The police have still been coming around, asking all of us questions, but they won't say whether or not they've got a suspect."

"Are you worried? You know, that the person who did that might be a lunatic and come after you?"

"Have you been talking to your father?"

"No. Katherine."

Stretching and yawing, Amelia wrapped her arms around her daughter, careful not to spill the coffee.

"No, sweetheart. The cops told all of us not to worry." That was a little white lie, but Amelia didn't think there was any harm if it set her daughter's mind at ease. Truthfully, she wasn't scared. It was a fluke, a weird occurrence. Aside from Ruth's strange comments, which could easily be written off as stress induced, this was just a tragedy—nothing more. There was no Jack the Ripper skulking around Food Truck Alley.

But when Monday came, the whole Alley was buzzing. The Burrito Wagon was closed, locked up tight with police tape all around it, and Mrs. Vega was sitting on the steps up to the truck, crying.

Chapter Eight

"Mrs. Vega? Are you all right?" Amelia asked.

"Oh, Amelia," she cried. "They take my nephew Matthew into custody."

"For what?"

"They say he killed that man." She sobbed into a white handkerchief. "They say because he fought with him that he must have killed him. My Matthew, he's not perfect. He's been in trouble, but he's a good boy."

Amelia couldn't help but remember all the tattoos on Matthew. One didn't have to be in the FBI to know those were gang tattoos. She hated herself for thinking it, but Mrs. Vega's nephew looked as if he ate nails for breakfast.

"He was with me every night last week. He's turning his life around—no more running with those bad people down in Los Angeles. He's even paying to have his tattoos removed. But the police see his record, and they make up their mind, just because he yelled at that man." She wiped her eyes. "Peter Indesh owed money. He owed us twenty-five dollars for food he didn't pay for. When Matthew ask him for it, he go crazy."

"People don't usually get killed for twenty-five dollars," Amelia mumbled to Mrs. Vega.

"No. My Matthew was with me every night. But the police don't believe me. I'm an old woman. I don't count. Without my nephew, I can't run this business. The police have it all taped up like the body was found inside." Her tears rolled down her brown, wrinkled cheeks. "What I do if I can't cook? Work at Walmart?"

Amelia didn't know Matthew, and Peter Indesh did argue with him, but even if the boy had wanted to kill Peter, he probably wouldn't have left the body within walking distance of his older aunt's food truck. That didn't add up.

"I'm so sorry, Mrs. Vega. If there is anything I can do..."

"What can you do? Matthew is in jail. I have to sell this truck to get money for a lawyer. The public defender won't help him. But I can't sell the truck because the police have it taped up. They find long knife in there. We don't even use knife like that. I tell them that is not ours, but I'm just an old lady. They won't even let me work."

Amelia patted the old woman's shoulder as Mrs. Vega leaned into her and sobbed.

Without telling Mrs. Vega anything, Amelia let the thoughts roll around in her head. Of course, Matthew could have gone out in the middle of the night when Mrs. Vega was asleep. But that was a pretty big maybe. And sure, people had been killed for less than twenty-five dollars, but usually, drugs or alcohol were involved. All the times Amelia had seen Matthew working, he looked totally alert and normal.

Not long afterward, Amelia saw Lila coming around the corner. She was hard to miss with a ten-gallon cowboy hat on. Amelia waved, getting Lila's attention, and she came right over. Lila told Mrs. Vega she was sorry after hearing the story.

"What are you going to do now?" Lila asked.

"Go home," Mrs. Vega said bitterly. "I take the bus and go back home. My daughter and granddaughter are coming by."

"Look, don't take the bus. Let me pay for a cab for you." Lila took some money from her purse and folded it into the old woman's hand. "It isn't a lot, but it's the least I can do. Take a cab. You'll get home quicker to see your family."

The old woman sniffled, nodded, and repeated gracias over and over as she left.

"That's just heartbreaking," Lila said. "And not to be selfish or anything, but those burritos were fantastic. Now the world will be deprived of a dish that could resolve disputes and bring peace to war-torn countries. Such a shame."

"Yeah," Amelia mumbled, her mind reeling. "It is a shame."

Throughout the day, Amelia's mind kept going back to what Mrs. Vega had said. Mr. Indesh had owed them twenty-five dollars. Mrs. Indesh had said Peter needed to pay his debts. She couldn't have been talking about twenty-five dollars for the Burrito Wagon.

After she cleaned up, she drove the truck home. The arrest of Mrs. Vega's nephew felt like a splinter stuck in her brain.

"Hey, Mom," Adam said as she walked in the front door.

He was coming from the kitchen, carrying a bag of chips, and the television was on in the front room. Some cartoon was playing, with wide-eyed girls and angular-haired boys fighting bizarre cryptids.

"Hi, honey," Amelia said. "Where's your sister?"

"Upstairs with Katherine. I think she's staying for supper."

"Oh, okay. Hey, I need your help."

"Sure." He picked up the remote control and shut off the television.

"If you wanted to find out about a person, how would you go about doing it?"

"Well, first I'd go to their Facebook page, and if that wasn't enough, I'd check the other social-media sites. I guess it all depends on how deep you want to go and how many rules you want to break."

"Oh, Lord. Please tell me you aren't breaking any rules. And by saying *rules*, you aren't hiding the fact you really mean *laws*."

"No. The Freedom of Information Act protects me in most instances."

"I don't want to know." Amelia sighed. "Okay. Peter Indesh. How would I find out about him?"

"Just wait."

Adam ran downstairs and within seconds was back in the kitchen with his laptop underneath his arm.

Chapter Nine

Adam sat down at the kitchen table. His fingers flew across the keyboard and within seconds pulled up a Facebook page that had been created by Peter Indesh.

"This is interesting," Adam said.

"What's that?"

"Well, he's only got twenty-seven Facebook friends."

"What does that mean?"

"When a person has over, say, a hundred Facebook friends, it is pretty safe to say they don't know all of those people personally. But, see here?" Adam pointed at the screen. "Peter has twenty-seven friends. Chances are he knows half of them personally."

"And what does that mean?"

"Well, I don't know yet. Let's see what they were talking to him about."

After a few more key punches, Adam was looking at Peter Indesh's Facebook page with all the entries from his twenty-seven friends.

"Now, look here. Some of these have kept coming, so whoever is posting them obviously doesn't know Peter that well, or they'd know he was dead."

"Makes sense."

"So you can probably cross them off your list of possible suspects."

"What are you guys doing?" Meg bounded down the stairs with her best friend Katherine following close behind her.

"Oh, your brother is just trying to show me how to work on my webpage for the Pink Cupcake," Amelia said. "Hi, Katherine."

She wanted to keep this information about her business from Katherine rather than from Meg. She was a sweet girl and a good friend to her daughter, but it was common knowledge that Katherine was a talker.

"Hi, Mrs. Harley. Sorry to hear about the gruesome events at your food truck."

"Oh, honey, it wasn't at my food truck. It was just near the food truck. Actually, it wasn't all that near. It was across the dining area."

"Some of the kids at school said it was like that one movie with the guy who skewered people with a sickle. Was it like that? Did it look like a horror movie? I'd be afraid to go back there. I've read that if a person is killed in, like, an unnatural way that their soul can't rest and they, like, haunt that place forever."

"It wasn't that bad, no."

"Remember that story we had to read in class about the guy whose mother married his uncle, and so her son murdered them both? That was creepy."

"Are you talking about *Macbeth*?" Adam asked, his eyebrows pushed together and his lips frowning.

"Yeah," Katherine said, nodding slowly, her eyes wide.

"Well, I am glad to see they are still teaching the classics at your high school," Amelia said. "Katherine, I wouldn't worry about ghosts if I were you. Are you staying for supper?"

"Is that okay, Mom?" Meg asked.

"Yeah, as long as you guys don't mind frozen pizza." Amelia ran a hand through her hair, pulling it back from her face. "I've actually got a slight headache, so you guys can feed yourselves, and I'm going to take a shower and lie down." She picked up Adam's laptop and folded it underneath her arm.

"What's for dessert?" Katherine whispered in Meg's ear.

"There are sugar lemon cookies with vanilla frosting in the fridge," Amelia called out as she went up the stairs to her bedroom. "They are a new creation, so let me know what you think, and I'll post it on my FB page."

Amelia heard the girls giggling with excitement as Adam teased them about being juvenile. He was only a year older than his sister, but he made sure she never forgot it.

Once upstairs with the bedroom door closed, Amelia set Adam's laptop on the bed and opened it. She got a pen and paper and wrote down all the names of the people listed as Mr. Indesh's friends.

Adam seemed to have been spot on. The names of the friends who were still tagging him on posts had no idea he'd never see their witty comments or political view-points. He'd never see the post about some local politician out of California who had just been indicted and whom Kyle Wilford wished a pox upon. Peter would also never see that Ami Grant had just gotten a new haircut.

It made Amelia pause for a moment. How sad it was that those people didn't know the story. She wondered if Ruth was going to put a stop to this and close down the account. That had to be something that could be done. Amelia had heard on the news about Facebook pages being shut down or incapacitated somehow.

Surely Ruth would do that for her late husband's Facebook page, right?

But as Amelia scanned the names and photos of the people Peter had "friended," she was surprised to see that his wife's name was missing from the list.

That's weird. Unless he's doing something she doesn't know about or he doesn't want her to know about.

Scrolling down, she saw many entries for gambling sites. He posted about winning at blackjack and poker, invitations to gambling events, tips on horseracing, and football pools.

"Everyone has hobbies. Heck, Katherine downstairs has seen every slasher film ever made, and she's never committed a crime," Amelia said aloud. "At least, I don't think so."

The page went on forever. Farther down, she read posts from Peter about taking things one day at a time and remembering that God had plans for everyone.

"He had a gambling problem," Amelia muttered.

It was obvious. She read his thoughts as they fought with each other. On one hand, he had mantras of encouragement to inspire change and strength. But on the other were the latest online gambling sites, video games you could win money on, and a whole host of blinking, glamorous articles and invitations to "win big" or "cash in."

"So he owed someone some money. And they probably were tired of waiting. That happens all the time in Vegas, Atlantic City... Heck, it probably happens in every city in every state. But Gary, Oregon?"

Chapter Ten

Taking a deep breath, she kept looking.

She could find nothing in any of the posts that would lead her anywhere else. He owed money, and that was that. Why should she continue? It was a dead end from here.

However, the image of Mrs. Vega sitting outside her food truck and sobbing pulled at Amelia's heart. She knew how easy it would be to turn a blind eye toward a child's bad behavior, especially when a parent might be so desperate to believe the child had changed his ways.

Had it been one of her children, she also would have insisted it wasn't either, even if Adam had the knife in his hand or Meg had the victim's blood on her shirt. She would simply have told the authorities to prove it. Mrs. Vega was no different.

Matthew looked like a troublemaker. But the fact that he looked like one and had a troubled history back in Los Angeles didn't make him automatically guilty.

After a few minutes of quiet thinking, Amelia snapped her fingers and picked up the phone next to her bed. As a single mother, she kept a landline in her house for emergencies. With lightning speed, she dialed a number she had memorized more than ten years before and called on a regular basis.

"Hey, girl! How's everything going?" Christine Mills chirped on the other end of the phone. "We just got back yesterday from a camping trip. Would you stop teasing your brother! Don't make me come over there!" she shouted at someone in the background. "I'm sorry. These savages belong in the wild, I swear. I don't care who started it! If I have to hang up this phone on your Aunt Amelia, you are going to be in big trouble."

Amelia laughed.

All the years she had known Christine, she had never threatened any kind of physical harm to one or all of her four boys or her husband. Truthfully, Amelia didn't think she'd ever laid a hand on any of them, but she had instilled a fear in all of them at an early age that you don't mess with Mama.

"Is it a bad time?" Amelia asked.

"Are you kidding? If I waited till it was a good time, I'd never talk to anyone. Thomas! That's it! Go sit in the corner! John, make sure he sits in the corner. If any of you talk to him, you're next! Okay, Amelia. I'm back."

"I have a question to ask you."

"I saw your truck on the news about that murder. Are you all right over there?"

"Yeah." Amelia sighed. "It's a weird scene, for sure. That is what I'm calling about, actually."

"Be quiet and go empty the dishwasher like I told you an hour ago! That's what you're calling about? Should I be worried?"

"Oh, no. I just need to know something. Do you still talk with Denise, Linda, and Sarah?"

There was dead silence on the other end of the phone for a moment.

"Yes, I still see them every once in a while. But you know after what they did to you, there is a considerable distance between us."

After the news of John's affair had been made public, Amelia went into seclusion, and Christine went on the warpath.

Gary, Oregon wasn't a booming metropolis, but it was a busy town. It had a Walmart, CVS drugs, and one of the last thriving bookstores in the entire state.

Reginald Books was a four-story bookstore so large it was listed in the *Guinness Book of World Records* as the largest collection of titles for a building that wasn't a library. It was so big tourists were often encouraged not to separate from each other, as it might take hours for them to be reunited. Their books covered every topic from the history of the gazebo to the life and times of pygmy warriors to how to create papier-mâché furniture, as well as the most recent Stephen King novel and the biography of the current secretary of state.

Like many of its dying competitors, such as Borders Books and Barnes & Noble, Reginald Books had a massive coffee shop that took up a good portion of the first level. Denise, Linda, and Sarah could be found there at least three times a week, sipping their frozen smoothies or iced teas, sitting on the same stuffed red couch and orange love seat near the front window, where they kept a close eye on who was coming and going.

Linda was the quietest of the three. She was older. She wasn't afraid to speak her mind but oftentimes, after she spoke, would feel guilty or uncomfortable with the words she'd just said. She would nervously twirl her big costume jewelry rings on her fingers when she had to eat crow.

Sarah was a pretty girl with strawberry-blond hair and braces at the age of thirty. She lived with her parents and had a steady boyfriend who was about to pop the question, and that was a fact she'd been stating for the past two years. She was a follower and a very faithful one at that.

Denise was the ringleader. She was married to Tom Giordano, a police officer who liked to talk in his sleep. It had been Denise's big idea to inform Amelia about

John at lunch. She seemed to relish watching the reactions of people when she dropped a particularly juicy piece of information in front of them, so much so that her eyes would narrow even as she smiled. With the backup of the Gary Police Department behind her, she was bolder than most women would be.

Their routines had not changed much since the Gatto's incident, and the reasoning behind their meetings also hadn't changed. They were the eyes and ears of Gary, Oregon.

It was there, as they took up space on that very red couch and that same orange love seat, that Christine had scolded them like children a year before.

"You were supposed to be her friend," Christine bellowed, paying no attention to the patrons staring in her direction. "And you do that to her in a public place? What kind of monsters are you?"

Denise stood up. "Who are you calling a monster?"

"You, Denise! I'm calling you a monster!" Christine, who just barely reached five foot two to Denise's five foot eleven, took a step closer, fearing nothing. "All three of you should be ashamed of yourselves! Absolutely ashamed!"

Nothing else was said as Christine left. However, less than twenty-four hours after that, Linda left a voice mail for Amelia, expressing her regret over how things had turned out and insisting that none of them had known about John "for very long." Amelia had never called her back.

"Why are you asking about those witches?" Christine asked. Something toppled over and broke in the background, but she didn't shout. She was too curious about Amelia's request.

"I was wondering if you could do me a solid."

"Anything. Of course."

"I was wondering if you wouldn't mind coming with me to Reginald Books to accidentally run into them."

"Do you mean with your car?"

Amelia laughed. "No. I mean to go in and play nice."

"Can I ask why you want to do this?"

"It's about this murder at Food Truck Alley. I just need a little information."

"Yeah, sure. Let me know when, and I'll be there. Whoever broke whatever broke is in so much trouble I can't even find words!" she yelled.

"Sorry, Mom" came in unison from the boys in the background.

"Can you go Saturday?" Amelia asked.

"Sure, as long as we can be back by two. Jay has got to see a guy about some chickens. Did I tell you we're buying chickens?"

"No. But I'll expect some free eggs," Amelia said without missing a beat. On the other end of the phone, she heard some yelling and what sounded like the youngest crying.

"I have to go. The animals need to be fed and turned out in the wild to run off some of their energy at baseball practice. I'll see you tomorrow."

Amelia hung up the phone and smiled. Christine had a way of making that happen.

After that tragic lunch with the girls, Christine had followed Amelia home. Once inside, she ran a hot bath for her and sat patiently on the closed toilet seat as Amelia cried and cried.

"Wash your face," she insisted after a long five minutes, handing Amelia a small white washcloth. "I'll get you some ice water while you dry off."

She had cut a lime and put the slices in the cold water, which she brought upstairs and handed to Amelia as she bundled herself in an old terrycloth robe that was anything but sexy or alluring.

"I gained weight, you know, after Meg was born," Amelia said. "They say once you hit forty, losing weight is almost impossible without surgery or spending hours and hours at the gym."

"This has nothing to do with your figure, Amelia," Christine said, tucking Amelia's hair behind her ears.

"I just get tired. Keeping up with the kids and this house is big. Sometimes, I'm just tired."

"I know."

"Why didn't he talk to me?" Amelia asked. "He could have told me he was unhappy. He could have said something, right?"

"Before you do anything, you have to get his side of the story. Look, the kids are going to be home in an hour or so, and John will be home tonight. Talk to him. See what he has to say."

"And what if it's all true? What if he has been unfaithful?"

"Well, I'll help you dig a hole in the yard, and then we can decide what to do from there."

Amelia giggled through her tears and hugged Christine tightly.

That night after she'd talked with John about the rumor she'd heard, he'd packed his suitcase and walked out the door, leaving her to explain to their children where he was going.

Snapping back into the present, Amelia went to the local news site on the computer and saw the latest details about what the press was calling the Food Truck Murder.

"How creative," she mumbled bitterly.

After scrolling down a couple of articles, she saw the mug shot of Matthew and the details of his arrest.

He was a seasoned criminal with ties to the Crips in Los Angeles.

He had a record that included breaking and entering, vandalism, and drug possession.

He was said to have been spotted lurking around the bushes the day before the grisly discovery was made.

So far, no weapon had been found, and the only motive was the dispute over a twenty-five-dollar tab.

"Does this sound right to you?" Amelia asked the computer.

It replied with dead silence.

Chapter Eleven

The next few days in Food Truck Alley were busy. Amelia wanted to give herself the day off on Saturday while the kids visited their father, so she worked hard to get all her cupcakes out the door and into the hands of customers.

On the Pink Cupcake webpage her son had created, Amelia had him offer a one-time coupon: buy one gourmet cupcake from the Pink Cupcake and get a second at half price. It worked better than she had anticipated, causing her to go home with empty reserves. Twice, she had to stop at the grocery store for more flour, almond extract, eggs, and half a dozen little niceties that made everyone recognize a Pink Cupcake cupcake.

All the while, her anticipation of Saturday was becoming more like an anxiety attack. She hadn't spoken to these women in more than a year other than the occasional curt hello or nod from her car.

She hated herself for feeling like such a wimp. But when she concentrated on why she was choosing that self-inflicted torture, that put things in perspective.

Mrs. Vega, the nicest lady a person could ever hope to meet, was all alone. The facts listed about the case were flimsy at best. But courts had convicted people for bigger offenses with less evidence.

She had to do something. With the list of names of the friends on Facebook tucked in her purse, Amelia met Christine at Reginald Books. Just as she had hoped, the girls were exactly where they were supposed to be, taking up the red couch and orange love seat, sipping their iced coffee drinks and chattering away like mad hens.

Amelia and Christine walked in their direction as if they didn't notice them. Then, with the dedication of an Oscar-hungry actress, Amelia stopped in her tracks, saw they were all looking at her, and she did the unthinkable. She smiled.

Nudging Christine, she pointed in their direction, and, following her friend's lead, even Christine managed a convincing smile.

"Look who it is!" Denise squealed, getting to her feet, smoothing out her blouse over her too-tight blue jeans and giving Amelia a hug plus a kiss on each cheek as the Europeans tend to do. "Amelia. How are you?"

Both Sarah and Linda followed her lead, getting to their feet and offering hugs as well. Christine gave very quick pats, as if she were hugging a trio of cactuses on a dare.

"I'm doing all right. How are you guys?" She pulled her purse off her shoulder and took a seat on the edge of the love seat next to Sarah, who affectionately rubbed her shoulder.

Christine sat next to Amelia on the arm of the love seat, keeping her mouth shut and her ears open just in case Amelia missed anything.

A few minutes of casual talk went by before Amelia asked the question she had been waiting to ask: "So, how about that murder at Food Truck Alley?"

It was like Pandora's Box had opened, and a flood of information from a dozen angles came rolling out of Denise's mouth.

"Well, you know that Peter and Ruth had been having problems for some time. They couldn't pay their bills. The house was about to be foreclosed on. They had one car repoed in the middle of the night. The Mercedes."

"No! I didn't know it was the Mercedes," Sarah whined as if that were the worst blow to the family.

"Yes, and I heard that Ruth had suspected Peter was having an affair." As soon as the words came out of her mouth, Denise froze.

Had it been a year or even six months before, Amelia would have had to excuse herself to go to the bathroom in order to bawl her eyes out in private. But she just sat calmly listening, as if the slip of the tongue had gone right over her head.

"Did she tell the police that?" Christine jumped into the conversation, rescuing Denise from her awkward moment.

"I don't know. But she said she had followed him one night to an abandoned-looking building and saw him meet a woman there."

"Who meets at an abandoned building to have an affair?" Sarah asked.

"Where was the warehouse?" Amelia asked innocently, looking each woman in the face.

"It was that place over on Steger Road, on the corner. It's across the street from Liona's Mane hairdresser place? The one with the big purple sign."

"Oh, yeah. I know which one you're talking about." Christine nodded.

"If that is the case, what about the suspect they have in custody?" Amelia scratched her head. She knew if Tom knew anything about the case, Denise would not be able to control herself. She'd spill it all.

"Have you seen that guy?" Denise asked. "He's absolutely huge. He looks like the Hulk."

"I heard he had a record and had dealings with the Oregon chapter of the Crips." Linda leaned in closer to join the conversation. She sounded funny using the term Crips. "He looks like a kneecap breaker."

Denise nodded her head enthusiastically, adding that that was the exact same thing Tom had said when they brought the guy in.

"Yeah, a real monster," Christine said, nodding innocently.

"You know, those gang members don't play around," Sarah said. "If you owe them money, they're going to collect. One way or another."

All three women lived in beautiful homes. Both Denise and Linda would inherit healthy pensions from their husbands' jobs, Denise from the Gary PD and Linda from the U.S. Post Office, where her husband had worked for almost forty years. Sarah's parents never asked her for anything and were probably counting the days they could shift her from their house to a husband's house.

None of them knew what it was like to see the cliff coming and know there was no way to stop.

Up until a year before, when the divorce papers were finally signed, Amelia hadn't known either. But she knew nice people when she met them. And Mrs. Vega was nice. But the cliff was quickly approaching her, and she needed help.

"Has anyone been to see Ruth?" Amelia asked. "The kids made her a dinner after we heard the news, but I just dropped it off and had to leave to get to work."

Denise leaned in. That was her signature move when she knew something good. "I stopped by to check up on her two days ago. She was on her laptop. I could see her through the lace of the curtain in the front door. She didn't move. Didn't look up. I'll bet she was searching his e-mail and finding heaven knows what."

"You mean she didn't come to the door? She didn't yell out or anything?"

"But I'm not going to go back there. It's none of my business."

Whether Denise knew more and wasn't saying or they had reached the bottom of the well, Amelia couldn't be sure. But she looked at her watch, unable to continue the façade any longer.

"Oh, gosh," she said. "Look at the time. Christine, we've got to hurry if we're going to get back in time for the kids' game."

Christine smacked her head with the palm of her hand.

"In all the excitement, I almost forgot. It was nice to see you ladies again." She stood, waved, and slowly backed up, baby step by baby step.

"It was nice seeing all of you." Amelia stood and waved.

"You should come to lunch with us sometime," Sarah said, her eyes blinking wildly, as though she had just come up with the greatest idea of all time.

"Maybe I will." Amelia thought she might need to squeeze them for information again. It had been her idea, after all, to play nice.

Chapter Twelve

Leaving the trio where they had found them, Amelia and Christine hustled to another end of the bookstore. Pulling her purse open, Amelia quickly pulled out a pen and scribbled down everything the girls had said.

"Why do I get the feeling you are taking me down a rabbit hole?" Christine asked.

"I'm not. I just needed a few minutes with them, and I was too much of a chicken to do it by myself."

"I feel so used."

"I'll make it up to you. How about lunch at Jack in the Box?"

"It's like we have one brain." Christine laughed.

They left the bookstore and had lunch, and Amelia dropped off Christine at her house, which was just three minutes from her house across the busy Haulsted Avenue.

"This was fun," Christine said. "Let's do it again some time when we don't have to visit the three witches from the story of Perseus."

"Christine, it's true. It really is like we have one brain."

From inside the house came a sound like something being thrown down a flight of stairs. Then they heard some steady hammering.

"Over there!" Christine's husband's voice boomed out the open front door. "Behind it!"

"Hey, Dad? Is this supposed to be peeling?"

"I should just run now," Christine said, shaking her head.

"Do you know what they're doing?"

"I asked them to vacuum while I was gone. Heaven only knows what is happening in there now." She blew a kiss to Amelia and marched off toward the house. After disappearing inside, she yelled, "What in the world?"

Backing slowly and quietly out of the driveway, Amelia drove to her own house. Adam's skateboard was propped against the front door. That was his signal that their dad had picked them up already.

The house would be quiet, fairly clean, and all hers until eight o'clock the next night. For the past several months, those had been the nights she would try some new recipes. The idea of a peanut-butter-and-jelly cupcake had still not left the back of her mind, and just to show Lila she was more valuable than just a bean counter, she thought she'd give the concoction a try.

A yellow cake would have been simple enough but perhaps with a raspberry extract for the cake and a subtle hint of peanut flavor mixed in. The idea of mixing in just a teaspoon of peanut oil with the cooking oil might have been either a disaster or one of the most brilliant ideas she'd had in her forty-four years of life. She wouldn't know until the timer went off.

The frosting would be pure homemade almond butter and homemade raspberry jam, swirled together so the contrasting light brown and dark magenta would look like a sweet on the board game Candy Land. She would also add a crumbled peanut-butter cookie on top of that.

It sounded fantastic.

"But can it be done?" she asked herself.

Just then, her cell phone rang. She pulled it from her back pocket and saw the caller was Meg. With flour-covered fingers, she tapped Accept and said, "Hi, honey. What's up?"

"Hi, Mom." Meg's voice was shaky.

"What's the matter?" Amelia's heart instantly began to race.

"I want to come home."

That was unusual. Ever since the split, Amelia had gone out of her way to make sure the children understood that the divorce had nothing to do with them. She insisted that she still loved their father—just in a different way. She pointed out how many blessings they'd received since everything had changed and that they would be okay as long as they all remembered to love each other.

"Did something happen?" Amelia asked.

"I just don't want to be here."

"Well, Meg, your dad looks forward to seeing you guys. He usually plans some good stuff, right? Did he plan anything tonight?"

"He and Adam went to the movies to see some nerdy sci-fi movie. I didn't want to go."

"Why do I get the feeling you're leaving something out?"

"He said he didn't like the Pink Cupcake," Meg said.

"What?"

"Adam went to the bathroom, and I was in the kitchen with Liza—"

"Liza was there?" Amelia knew it was petty and juvenile, but knowing that girl, only ten short years older than Meg, was around her children made her stomach flip.

"Yeah. I guess she's here all the time, now. I saw her clothes in Dad's room."

"Okay, honey. Well, we can't worry about that. So what did your dad say that has you so upset?"

"So I was in the kitchen, and I asked Dad if he saw your truck on the news. He said everyone saw that truck on the news, and he hated it."

Without letting Meg know that pleased her immensely, Amelia took a deep breath and tried to talk her daughter away from the ledge.

"Look, honey. Your dad works really hard. He deals with patients who have lots of mental issues, and it has got to wear him down at times. He says that because he doesn't know anything about it. That's all. He doesn't know how much fun we had painting it and picking the design. He doesn't know how many times we tried our recipes or how many people we had to interview before Miss Lila came along. He just doesn't know what he doesn't know. Ya know?"

"But why would he say that?"

"I don't know, honey. But I love the Pink Cupcake, and it would take something more than a comment by your overworked dad to get me to leave her."

"Yeah, okay."

"Don't feel bad. And don't tell your father you wanted to come home. Just have a nice time, and you'll be home in your own bed tomorrow night. Okay?"

"Okay. I love you, Mom."

"I love you, too."

"And I love the Pink Cupcake and can't wait until I can work there with you."

"If that's the case, summer vacation, hurry up and get here!" Amelia said.

Meg giggled on the other end of the phone before one last good-bye.

After setting the phone down on the counter, Amelia went back to her new recipe.

She did love the Pink Cupcake, and John was not going to ruin it as he had their marriage.

She wanted to yell and scream and cry, but instead she just stood still and looked out the window, her eyebrows pursed together and her lips pinched into an angry slit. Then she remembered Mrs. Vega.

"There are real issues in the world, John. You don't need to invent them."

As the sun was setting outside, the temperature of the house felt like an Arizona resort, so Amelia decided to leave all the windows open and the ceiling fans on and get out for a little while.

Ever since her conversation with the girls, she'd wanted to drive by the building on the corner of Steger Road across from the beauty salon with the purple sign. She could vaguely recall it.

"Probably because your eyes automatically go to that tacky purple thing," she mumbled, "They could be burning people at the stake over there, and you'd still just see the purple sign, wondering if you needed a haircut." She wiped her forehead with the back of her hand and grabbed her keys and purse.

Outside, the air was cool and moist. She looked up and saw no stars, as the clouds had rolled in. Gary, Oregon, was in the path of a few showers that night.

After climbing into her beater car, just an old used sedan she'd been able to get from Christine's husband's brother for a song, she started it up and backed out of the driveway, careful not to swing too close to the Pink Cupcake, sitting like a princess in the driveway.

The sedan was a blah cream color with red interior. The windows were manual, and it had no CD player. But the mileage was good, it only took twenty-five dollars to fill the tank every two weeks, and since she was driving the Pink Cupcake to work every day, the miles would hover around seventy thousand miles for a little longer.

She drove to the part of town where this building was supposed to be. After finding a place to park on the street a couple blocks away, she grabbed her umbrella from the back seat and headed in the direction of the nearly blinding purple sign, which read Liona's Mane.

It was a little after ten, a fact that had escaped Amelia, as it usually did when she was baking. She'd left the house thinking it was around seven. So when she saw some of the strange characters heading in and out of the liquor store on the next block, she was surprised.

That neighborhood wasn't awful, but it was rough around the edges. Twenty-four-hour currency exchanges, title loans, White Castle, and open-late McDonald's didn't attract the most stellar pillars of the community.

Amelia, wearing a sweat suit that complimented her figure, stood out a little more than she would have liked. Why she hadn't thought to just slip into a pair of jeans and an oversized T-shirt like usual, she wasn't sure. But she was out there, and she wasn't going to go back home just to change clothes.

"I heard she had it in her pocket."

"I don't know. But when she got there, it was gone."

"Did you hear that Karey is going to have a baby?"

"Another one? Didn't Ray just get laid off?"

The snippets of conversation of people perched on their darkened stoops were as varied as the people voicing them. An occasional whistle came Amelia's way, but she didn't pay any attention. They were kids, young men who couldn't see in the dark that she was old enough to be their mother.

As she neared the building, she saw a couple of lights on. First, there was a back door that had a lonely single light giving off an eerie green glow illuminating a circle around the door but leaving everything else in pitch darkness.

Up top on what would've been the second floor was another light, coming through a small window.

Finally, the front door was lit by a porch light, dim at best. If it was giving off forty watts, that was a lot. A man walked inside. He was wearing a baseball hat, so she couldn't see his face—not that she'd know him. She didn't know anyone from around there.

As she neared the door, she wondered what she would do when she got to it. Should she go in? That would be pretty nervy to just walk into some place where she had no business. Or should she just peek in? Maybe she should just watch and see if anyone else went in.

Before she could decide, she was in front of the door. Not wanting to look like some crazy loitering around in the darkness, she pulled open the door and stepped inside.

Chapter Thirteen

The featureless building had a strange smell, like mothballs and ammonia. The walls were plain beige institution-style bricks, and the floor was a lifeless white tile with specks of gold and brown, making only the most generic attempt at looking like marble.

Following the plain hallway, Amelia saw a sign on red construction paper, the only splash of color around. It was taped next to an open door, also a light-beige fake wooden thing with a large window, the kind of door in almost every classroom in the country. Written on the construction paper in black marker were the words Gamblers Anonymous.

People were already inside when Amelia peeked in. Some were already seated randomly in the five rows of folding chairs. Others were gathered around a snack table, where Amelia saw something she absolutely hated: two open packages of store-bought cookies. They were the Oreo kind, one with chocolate cookie and one with vanilla cookie. Store-bought cookies were tools of the devil, for sure. Amelia shook her head and pursed her lips.

Snapping out of her critique of the Gamblers Anonymous snack table, she carefully scanned the faces as best she could. Should she go in and take a seat? Should she hang back and observe from the back of the room? Should she leave altogether because that was a private meeting for people with real problems?

"Okay, everyone want to take a seat?" someone said loudly. The stout fellow, wearing a blue-and-white-striped button-down shirt, walked to the front of the group.

"Miss, we're getting started," said another man with gray hair and a mustache, leaning out the door and ready to pull it shut. "You coming in?"

Amelia nodded and quickly stepped into the room. She quietly took a seat at the end of the last row of chairs. The man with the gray mustache sauntered up the middle aisle and sat in the front row.

Suddenly, an uncomfortable feeling settled over Amelia. She shouldn't have been there. She felt as though she was spying. Pretending to suffer from an addiction might not have been a crime, but it was certainly immoral. It was as though she had crashed a wedding, gotten a plate full of food and a glass of champagne in her hands, and then realized there were no open seats. She held her breath.

"Hi, everyone. My name is Walter, and I suffer from a gambling addiction," said the man in the blue-and-white shirt.

No one waved or called out "Hi, Walter" as people did in the Al-Anon meetings. Everyone just sort of sat there.

"I see quite a few familiar faces and a few new ones." He nodded in a couple directions but didn't seem to notice Amelia, for which she was grateful. "For those of you that are new, I'll give you a little introduction. This is a safe place. You can talk freely about your problem as a compulsive gambler, or if it's a loved one that is addicted, you can vent here, too. We aren't here to judge."

He rubbed the back of his neck and told his story. He began with the night he'd gone into his nine-year-old daughter's room and, while she was sleeping, took her piggy bank from her dresser. After tucking it under his arm, he left the room, went into the garage, and cracked it open with a hammer. She had a total of seventeen dollars and thirty-eight cents. He spent it all on instant games, winning a total of fifty dollars. He took that money to a bar that had video slots and was up three hundred dollars when he bet it all and crapped out.

"That was seven years ago," he said.

Amelia was really only half listening as she studied the backs of the heads of everyone there. She couldn't very well go up to all the people and ask if they killed Peter Indesh. Plus, that was supposed to be an anonymous meeting. The folks there might not have known each other's names. There could've been six Peters in there.

"Before we get started with the testimonials, I'd like to take a minute to remember our friend Peter. As you know, he died in a senseless act of violence just a couple of days ago. Let's pray to our higher power that his family finds peace."

So much for having to be sneaky. They knew Peter. Several people nodded.

But an uncontrollable sniffling and sobbing caught Amelia's attention. At the end of the second row on the opposite side of the room was a blonde wearing a sheer flowery top. She was dabbing her eyes with a tissue and flipping her long locks behind her as she did.

"He was a wonderful man." She choked the words out too loudly. "It's a real loss." She cried dramatically as the man with the gray mustache rushed to her with a bottle of water.

Watching her, Amelia couldn't help but think she looked familiar. But without seeing her from the front, she couldn't be sure.

Was this the woman that Peter's wife Ruth saw him with? If only she could see her face. Amelia was shocked to see the woman took a good ten minutes to calm down. Finally, after multiple sips from the bottle of water, the blonde regained her composure. Was she going to give a testimonial? Would she stand up and introduce herself to the room?

Come on. What are you waiting for?
Amelia shifted in her seat.

The minutes ticked by as another woman, in her late sixties, told the story of how she'd caught her husband rifling through her purse for money. He had no idea she had resorted to keeping her money in her hidden bra purse.

The old woman was followed by a young man, about twenty, who said he'd driven to Portland with the intention of hitting an off-track betting facility, but when he had gotten there, he realized he not only didn't have any cash but had forgotten his debit card. He had no credit cards, as they were maxed out already.

"It was my higher power telling me, 'Not tonight.'" he said, smiling from ear to ear.

Everyone clapped for him, even Amelia, who thought, Atta boy as he took his seat, his cheeks bright red.

Finally, the meeting came to an end with everyone reciting the Serenity Prayer. Amelia tried to linger, but the blonde was not moving. She was staying in her seat.

Not wanting to be questioned or cornered, Amelia stood, clutched her purse tightly to her shoulder, and, with one last glance at the blonde, left the room. Some of the people watched her as she walked out, trying to give a friendly smile or a nod of solidarity, but she kept her eyes low.

She stepped outside. The rain was coming down harder. She saw a clump of bushes just outside the circle of light from the porch lights. Amelia quickly ducked into them and watched the door as rain saturated her hair and sweat suit.

People filed out and went in opposite directions. Some shook hands. Other people gave each other hugs. But there was no blonde to be seen.

"This is crazy," Amelia mumbled, wiping her eyes.

Finally, the door swung open, and the man with the gray mustache walked out with the blonde next to him. They spoke in very low whispers. Had it been a clear night, Amelia would have been able to hear what they were saying. But the rain pounding on the sidewalk drowned out every syllable.

The older man was saying something while looking down at his shoes as he stood underneath the awning, shaking his head the whole while.

Then it was the blonde's turn to shake her head. Her mannerisms reminded Amelia of a teenager trying to get a parent to agree to something.

But whatever the topic was, the older man was not agreeing. He put his hands up in the universal surrender pose then walked back into the building, leaving the blonde standing there.

Still, Amelia couldn't see her face. She had popped open an umbrella, which covered her entire torso in shadow. Amelia couldn't hear the woman's voice. She was simply sure she had seen the woman somewhere. Her form was familiar. Her hair was familiar. But as hard as Amelia tried to sort the files of faces in her mind, she couldn't grasp it.

Dashing back to her car, she hoped she wouldn't catch pneumonia. Amelia wondered what else she could do. She felt a dead end quickly approaching.

"A hot shower and a good night's sleep. Think about it tomorrow. Tomorrow, you'll have an answer." She nodded as she pulled her beater car into the driveway of her home. Then she put the car in park, climbed out, ran through the rain to the front door, and let herself in.

The house smelled fresh and felt cool after the oven having been on for so long. Checking her phone, which she'd set to silent, she saw no more messages from Meg or Adam. Everything must have been okay at their father's house.

If she wanted to, Amelia could've worked herself up into a frenzy over what John had said in front of Meg. But she put it out of her mind.

Regardless of the fact that she knew she'd seen that blond woman somewhere but couldn't place her, there was obviously something between her and Peter. Of course, letting her mind drift toward the gutter, she realized they might have been sharing a bed. But maybe it was something less sordid. Maybe they were each other's support system. Maybe they talked together, or perhaps Peter had helped the blonde at one time when she had nowhere else to go.

After pulling off her wet clothing and standing underneath hot streams of water in her shower, Amelia was struck with an idea.

"Matthew. I'll pay him a visit. Mrs. Vega can't afford bail, so he's just sitting in the jail in town. I'll go tomorrow." After stepping out of the shower and covering herself in her thick pink terrycloth robe, she wrapped her head in a towel, made the rounds to check all the windows and doors, and headed to the end of the hall to her bedroom.

The house she lived in wasn't nearly as fancy as the house she'd shared with John during their marriage. But every day, Amelia came to love it more and more. The first night she'd stayed there, she waited for the kids to fall asleep then cried quietly in what seemed a very lonely, cold double bed.

It wasn't that she missed John all that much. Honestly, she had felt the draft getting colder and colder every time he walked past her without looking at her. She missed the idea of being with someone—not necessarily John, but someone.

Now, when she stretched on her bed and snapped on the television, she enjoyed the space, the freedom, the ability to watch a movie without someone coming in and snapping to another channel just to check a score or hear the headlines. She loved her children, but the quiet was nice. Come the following night, she'd be ready for her kids to come home and tell her what they did with their father.

She fell asleep with a black-and-white movie playing on the classic-movie station. She had never heard of that one, but Bette Davis played a vindictive, conniving spoiled girl who caused a car accident but tried to hide from it, begging her rich uncle to protect her.

When Amelia woke up, the credits were rolling up the screen.

She clicked off the television, turned onto her side, and took a deep breath, smelling the sweet scent of her clean sheets.

Tomorrow, she'd go to jail.

Chapter Fourteen

"Can't you wait until I get home? I want to go, too," Meg told her mother over the phone.

"Honey, I'm just stopping to visit Mrs. Vega's nephew." Amelia fussed with the cuff of her shirt as she got dressed for work. "I am going to go straight after work."

"But I've never seen the inside of a police station."

Amelia smiled and shook her head, wondering whether John was within earshot of her conversation with Meg. That would be all he'd need to hear.

"I'll arrange a field trip to the Gary Police Station when you get back, okay?"

"I guess. Do you want to talk to Adam?"

"Yes, just for a second."

"Hi, Mom," her son said.

"Hey, honey. I need to look on your computer again. Do you mind if I venture into your cave and use your desktop?"

Amelia wanted to respect Adam's privacy. As the only male in the house, he was destined to do some things differently. He kept clean laundry and dirty laundry in separate piles, but they didn't always make it to their designated drawers or hangers or baskets. Dishes from late-night snacks often found refuge on his bookcase shelves or on his nightstand, and there were CDs of music, videos, and games stacked to various heights on the floor around his desk.

"Sure, Mom. Go ahead. Do you need me to help you with anything?"

"No. I'm just looking up something on Pinterest is all."

"Did Meg say you were going to jail?"

"Yes, but just to visit Mrs. Vega's nephew. Please don't discuss it around your father. He will... get worried or something."

"Yeah, sure."

"Okay, I'll see you guys tonight, then. Be good and have fun."

Before hopping into the big pink truck, Amelia ventured down to the basement to use Adam's desktop computer.

After removing a pile of clothes from the wheeled chair in front of the computer and placing them on Adam's unmade bed, Amelia took a seat and tapped the keyboard. The image of a hulking creature appeared, a chainsaw in one hand and a shotgun in the other. Obviously, it was some monster from one of the video games he was playing or creating.

She wasn't exactly sure what she was doing but managed to pull up the Facebook page of Peter Indesh. It was still up, and things had not changed much. The posts that were new were superficial comments and articles by "friends" who didn't know of his untimely death.

There was nothing there.

However, on a whim, Amelia typed in Ruth Indesh's name. What she saw made her do a double take. At the top of the posts was a trip to Las Vegas. Ruth was planning a trip within the next week.

"Really? Has the body even been buried yet?" Amelia mumbled, frowning at the screen. Checking the clock, she realized she didn't have any more time to search Ruth's posts. But that was something she found unsettling.

"Hmm, I did leave a dish with her. Maybe I should stop by there, too."

It was going to be a very busy day.

* * *

That turned out to be true in more ways than one. Once Amelia arrived at Food Truck Alley and parked the truck, Lila came sauntering up.

"Hey, girl," she said, stepping up to the driver's-side door. "How's it going?"

Amelia looked at Lila and smiled. "I'm good. And you?"

"Well, I am doing just fine. I was paid a visit by Gary's finest men in blue last night."

"What? Why?" Amelia asked.

She and Lila went through what had become their morning routine of snapping on the ovens, folding the pink boats to hold the cupcakes, getting the day's ingredients organized, and then mixing everything together, all the while discussing whatever had surfaced. In that case, it was a visit from the police.

"They were just following up. Detective Walishovsky asked me if I had had any run-ins with Matthew or people who might be associates of his."

"What did you tell him?"

"I told him that Matthew was the kind of guy a woman my age wanted around. He was big and scary looking and rarely spoke but could cook. Truthfully, suspicion of murder aside, if I were twenty years younger, I'd be batting my eyes in his direction."

Amelia laughed.

"They also asked about you."

"Really."

"Yes, and they said they had tried to contact you but got no answer."

"No. I was out last night." Amelia couldn't bring herself to tell Lila she had crashed a Gamblers Anonymous meeting. That sounded so pitiful. "There were a few things I needed from the store for home. The kids were with their father, so I got some errands out of the way." She hated lying to Lila. Her gut told her Lila could be trusted with just about anything, but she didn't want to put Lila in a position where she'd have to lie. It was better to leave out the gory details.

When all the food trucks were up and running and people lined up outside the truck, Amelia's mind raced as she thought of what she was about to do after work.

Like Meg, Amelia had never been in a police station, either. Not only was she going to the police station, but she was going to visit someone charged with murder. She hated to admit it, but it was kind of exhilarating.

"My gosh," Lila finally said at closing time. "Why does it feel like there were a thousand more customers today than there were yesterday? Please don't tell me that's how old age sets in, that it just falls on top of you all of a sudden, and the next thing you know, you're browsing for Hoverounds or walkers with the tennis balls at the bottom."

"It felt like that because I think there were more. What do the receipts say?"

Lila finished up the paperwork and smiled. "A few more days like this, and you're looking at early retirement."

"If I weren't so tired, I'd be jumping for joy." Amelia sat down on one of the metal ledges on the opposite side of the ovens, away from the door. "And I meant to tell you I made peanut-butter-and-jelly cupcakes last night."

"Really? And how did they turn out?"

"Delicious. I think you've come up with a real hit. I'll be happy to pay you a finder's fee or something if you can give me some time to get a clearer picture of—"

"You'll do no such thing. With those two cute kids of yours, one being a boy who will just start to eat more and more the older he gets... No. You keep your money. I am happy to help. And I'll be happy to eat a couple prototypes, too."

"You're the best, Lila."

"Yeah, I know. So, what are you doing tonight? Anything good?"

"I can't shake this murder."

"I know, right? I feel just awful for Mrs. Vega," Lila said.

"I was thinking of going to the jail tonight and talking with Matthew Rodriguez." Amelia waited for Lila's reply.

It was not what she expected.

"Can I come, too?" Lila asked.

"You sound like my daughter."

"Look, there is something fishy about the whole thing. That Detective Walishovsky left a very bad taste in my mouth. I didn't want to say anything, but do you know he was very interested in some weird things? He wanted to know how long we had worked together, how long we knew each other... I wasn't sure what that was all about, but you know when something just doesn't sit right with you. That didn't sit right with me."

"I don't ever pretend to know what it's like to be a cop," Amelia said. "It's got to be one of the hardest jobs out there. But I'm worried these guys are just taking the easy way out, and maybe Matthew is just a convenient scapegoat. Or I could be completely wrong, and he's a compulsive liar and murderer." Amelia shook her head and ran her hands through her hair. "Something has been nagging me since the beginning, and I just can't seem to shake it."

"Go with your gut," Lila said, her face serious. "Is your gut telling you to bring me with you?"

Amelia laughed and nodded.

Chapter Fifteen

The jail cells in the Gary Police Department were located in the basement. When Amelia and Lila walked in, they immediately felt the heavy gaze of the officer behind the thick glass at the front desk. She was a younger woman and wore her dark-brown hair in a ponytail. She looked suspicious of everyone.

"Hi," Amelia said. "I'm not sure how to go about this, but I'd like to visit one of the prisoners you have. Matthew Rodriguez."

"Visiting hours are from nine a.m. to four p.m.," the woman said matter-of-factly.

"How is anyone who works supposed to be able to visit a loved one during those hours?" Lila inquired politely.

"They make arrangements," the officer said. "I'm sorry. Unless it is an emergency, I can't really do anything about it."

"Look, I really think that Matthew Rodriguez is innocent. I just want to talk to him for a minute. This isn't Leavenworth Prison. This is the Gary Police Department. Isn't there someone who I can talk to who might be willing to bend the rules for just a second? I won't take five minutes."

The officer looked at Amelia. "Wait here." She pushed herself up from the desk and turned around. After walking past a couple cubicles, she disappeared through a door at the back of the office.

Within a few minutes, she returned with Detective Walishovsky and marched up to the front desk.

"Which one of you wants to see the prisoner?" he asked.

Amelia raised her hand meekly.

There was a loud buzz from the left, indicating the door had been unlocked. The detective pulled the door open and waved Amelia in.

"I'll wait right here," Lila whispered.

Amelia went through the door and jumped as the heavy lock slipped back into place, locking her in with the police.

"Thank you for making this allowance for me to meet with Mr. Rodriguez," she said. "I'm sorry it is outside the normal visiting hours, but I work, and—"

"I know who you are, Mrs. Harley." The detective handed her a badge that said Visitor and hung on a ribbon.

She slipped it over her head, and her gut twisted inside her.

"Yes, sir?" she said, waiting for him to finish and explain what he meant.

But he didn't say another word. Instead, he led her to another door that led to a gray stairwell. When they descended the metal steps, their footsteps *clank, clang, clanked* all the way down. The temperature seemed to dip a couple of degrees, too. *Or maybe I'm just nervous.*

They were at the head of a long corridor next to a uniformed officer who had been sitting at a wide desk in the center.

"She's here to see Rodriguez," the detective grumbled. "She's got five minutes."

The officer nodded and stood from the desk. He reached to his right, pulled out a folding chair, and walked down the corridor to the very end.

Before she could follow, the detective took her arm firmly. "We've got a few rules here."

"I'm good with rules, Detective. You don't need to take my arm." She pulled free and stood rail straight, looking up at the detective.

"One: you do not touch or reach for the prisoner at all. Two: you do not attempt to pass any kind of material to the prisoner at all. Three: if you choose to ignore these rules, you'll have the cell next to this prisoner. Do you understand my rules?"

"Yes." She was terribly shaken but held herself in check so as not to show any fear.

Amelia looked to her left and right, expecting to see a hundred different scary images of convicts that she had seen in movies, but there were only the three cells, two completely empty.

With a loud clang and scrape across the cement floor, the officer set up the chair more than an arm's distance in front of the cell. "Five minutes!" he said loudly, his voice echoing in the empty cell block.

Amelia took her seat and looked into the cell.

Matthew had been on his bed, but when he contorted his neck to look upside down, he smiled. "Hello, Mrs. Harley. What are you doing here?" He lifted his massive body off the bed with ease and took a seat at the edge of his bunk, next to the bars.

Wearing just a T-shirt and pants, with all those tattoos, he was indeed a menacing figure. But Amelia admitted to herself she could see traits of his aunt in his face. They had the same brown, almost black eyes and the same double chin.

"Since I've only got five minutes I'll cut to the chase," she said. "I think you're innocent. I've been looking into some things that seemed odd to me. But I don't have any solid proof. Is there anything you can tell me? Is there any way you can prove you were with your aunt other than your word?"

"I wish I could. I don't want to be in this place. But the truth is I went home after work with my aunt. We ate dinner, watched television. I said my prayers and turned in early. Working that food truck is exhausting."

"Has your aunt been in to visit?"

"Sí. Yes, she has."

"She told me they found a weapon, Matthew."

"Yeah, that's bogus, too. It could have been from anyone. We are next to trucks that carve a dozen different meats every day. It could have come from any of those. But they are sure it is me because of my tattoos." He looked down at his arms, which he stretched out in front of him. Splaying his fingers, he shook his head.

"Can you tell me what kind of knife it was?"

"I was told it was a long knife like this." He held out his fingers about twelve inches apart. "We don't even have knives like that. Our burritos are made with beans. My aunt uses a small steak knife to cut her vegetables. She's done it like that her whole life." He took a deep breath. "That guy, Mr. Indesh, owed money all over. My aunt, she's such a softy. She won't let a man go hungry. But too many take advantage. Not so much since I was there, but they tried. He owed her twenty-five dollars. It doesn't sound like a lot, but that was a week's worth of tomatoes. That is half a tank of gas. We need that money. We aren't rich. And when he came begging again for another handout, well, I don't care if his wife gambles his paycheck away. That isn't my problem."

"His wife gambled?"

"Yes. That was what he was saying to anyone who'd listen. His wife had a gambling problem. She had sunk them in debt. He didn't know what to do to get her to stop."

Amelia sat there as if she'd been slapped.

Matthew looked at his hands and shook his head again. "Mrs. Harley, I did some bad things when I lived in LA. But I never killed anyone. When I looked at the men around me, I didn't want to be them." Matthew took a deep breath. "I had a father who died in Afghanistan. Most of them didn't know their dads. My sisters both graduated from high school. Most of their sisters were in girl gangs or pregnant. Everyone I was around was so filled with hate. I just didn't have it. So I left and came here. I thought it would be better. I was getting all my art removed from my skin." Again, he looked at his arms as if he wished they weren't his. "I know what people think when they see me. But I'm no killer."

"One minute, Ms. Harley!"

Both Amelia and Matthew looked in the direction of the officer who'd shouted.

"I believe you, Matthew," she said. "What does your lawyer say?"

"He says because of my history that it will be hard to prove I was home the whole night–that it will be easy for the prosecution to say I snuck out or my aunt is covering for me."

Amelia shook her head. "That still sounds really flimsy to me."

"Yes, to you it does because you know my aunt and are a kind person. Put me in front of twelve strangers who don't know any of us, and they'll see what they want to see."

"Time's up, Ms. Harley."

"I have to go, Matthew. Don't give up hope. Will your aunt be coming to see you?" she asked while standing and folding up the chair.

"Yes, she and my cousin and her daughter come every day."

"Good. Don't give up, Matthew. The truth has a way of coming out."

He smiled, stood, and waved a weary goodbye.

Amelia carried the folding chair to the end of the corridor, where the police officer took it from her and set it back in the corner, where it would wait until another visitor showed up.

"Just go back up the stairs?" She pointed shyly toward the metal steps. In a place like that, she didn't want to do anything to rock the boat. The last thing she wanted was the Gary Police Department thinking she was some sort of troublemaker.

The policeman nodded. "Give your badge back to the detective."

"Thank you, Officer."

He nodded. "Have a good night, ma'am."

Amelia climbed the stairs, sure everyone in the whole facility could hear her coming. Before she reached the door, it clicked and opened. Detective Walishovsky was there with his hand out. His steely gray eyes had years of police experience behind them, and Amelia thought they looked very suspicious not only of Matthew but of her, too.

"Badge."

Amelia slipped it over her head and handed it to him.

"Thank you again for your assistance, Detective."

"I know it's hard to see someone we care about in a situation like this," he said, his back straight and shoulders back.

Had she had a criminal nature, Amelia would have been easily intimidated by the detective.

"Especially when they're innocent." Her voice was sad.

"That's the good thing, Ms. Harley. We are all innocent until proven guilty."

He led her through the office of cubicles, back to where Lila was chitchatting through the thick glass with the officer at the desk. They seemed to have become fast friends. That was easy to do with Lila. She had a charm that just drew people in.

"Thank you, again," Amelia muttered as she quickly pushed past him while he held the heavy metal door.

"If there is anything else I can help you with, Ms. Harley..." He didn't smile. He didn't even smirk. All he did was nod in her direction.

"It was nice talking with you, Darcy. Thanks for everything," Lila said, waving to the officer behind the glass. "All the best to you and your fiancé."

Officer Darcy waved and wished them both a good night.

"So, did you learn anything?" Lila pulled her purse over her shoulder.

"Sounds like *you* did."

"Yeah, Darcy is getting married in about a month to another officer she met in cadet training. Isn't that sweet? So tell me what you found out."

"Well, the first thing will rock your world. Peter Indesh didn't have a gambling problem. His wife was the one with the gambling problem."

"I had no idea. That is something. Are you sure it wasn't a ruse—him passing off the blame and shame of his own behavior just to make himself look better?"

"I don't think so." Amelia still didn't want to tell Lila she had sneaked into the GA meeting. It sounded so desperate. She continued relaying the other facts. "The knife they said they found in the Burrito Wagon was a big knife, Matthew said. He said his aunt never uses anything larger than a steak knife to cut veggies, and their burritos are bean."

"That is queer."

"But he doesn't have any alibi the detective is willing to believe."

"Well, one thing is for sure, that detective has eyes for you," Lila said.

"What?" Amelia nearly choked on the air she was breathing.

"Oh, you don't have to be a detective to pick up on those clues."

"Are you crazy? He grabbed me by the arm like this when he was giving me instructions." She took Lila's arm and demonstrated the detective's behavior.

"Okay, you are going to visit a guy they think committed a murder. They have rules so you don't get hurt. Seems to me he was extra concerned about you being down there. Did he stay and listen to your conversation?"

"No. He went back upstairs."

"See? He gave you privacy. Yup. I'm usually not wrong about these things."

"Well, I think you are off your rocker. I'm not interested. I've got too much on my plate as it is."

"Yeah, who in their right mind would want a tall, handsome detective on the police force interested in them? Icky."

"What?"

Lila giggled and bumped Amelia with her hip.

"Well, let me give you a lift home and–"

"Oh no, honey. You go on ahead. I'll hail a cab."

"Lila, you are making me very suspicious. Please don't tell me you're doing this because you live in a box or in an abandoned building or something and are embarrassed."

Lila tossed her head back and laughed out loud. "I assure you I don't live in a cardboard box. Not yet, anyways." She slipped her arm through Amelia's. "Your kids will be coming home soon. You should get home before them. If you drop me off, you might not make it. Please, I'm fine out here on my own."

"Okay." Amelia suspiciously eyed her friend. "But I'm inviting myself over for coffee one of these days. You won't be able to stop me."

Lila laughed again. She watched Amelia climb into her big pink truck and back out of the parking spot.

"See you in the morning?" Amelia called.

"You bet."

Chapter Sixteen

On her way home, Amelia looked at her watch and saw she had about half an hour before the kids would be arriving home. That gave her just enough time to stop at the Indesh address and ask for her dish back.

She pulled up to the house, half expecting Ruth to be sitting on the porch swing again, rocking and babbling nonsense about messes and such.

Instead, she saw a house with every light on inside.

Looking around, Amelia didn't see any other cars to indicate Ruth had visitors. The place gave off a weird glow in the dusk, as if a UFO might've been inside.

Amelia walked up to the door and rang the doorbell. At first, she didn't hear anything, but then there were footsteps, slow and deliberate, pounding on the wooden floor. Ruth appeared, distorted and fractured by the etched glass in her door. Pulling the door open, she received Amelia with half a smile.

"Hi, Ruth. I was just checking in to see how you were."

Amelia thought she looked tired. That was to be expected.

"Hi, Amelia. I'm glad you came by. I was about to venture over to your place and bring you back your dish. Come on in."

Looking at her watch, Amelia saw she still had about twenty minutes. She decided to look around, get a feel for things, and then go. She wasn't Sherlock Holmes, after all. She couldn't tell by a smudge of charcoal and a piece of gum wrapper who the killer was.

"Please tell the kids that their spaghetti was delicious." Ruth picked the dish up off the dining-room table, leading Amelia to believe she had intended to bring it back.

"I will." Amelia took the dish and held it with both hands. "How are you, Ruth?"

"I'm fine. The insurance money was delivered almost immediately, and that took care of quite a few of the things that had been worrying us."

"Not a good way to collect, though."

"No. But we would have parted sooner or later. He just made someone madder than me, is all." Ruth looked at Amelia sadly.

"You know, they have a man in custody."

"Yes, I know. Mrs. Vega's relative. She came by the house, asking for me to tell the truth, and..." Ruth shut her mouth tightly and appeared to be biting her tongue. "I'm expecting some people, Amelia. Tell the kids thanks, again."

Amelia stood there for a second. Ruth obviously wanted to confess something. Did she kill her own husband? It was possible. It happened all the time. But Amelia couldn't imagine Ruth overpowering Peter. And what were they doing in Food Truck Alley? It didn't make sense.

"Ruth, if there is anything I can do... If you just need someone to talk to, you can trust me."

Ruth looked at Amelia as if she were trying to see something behind her eyes. "I know that, Amelia. I know what those other women did to you when John was cheating. They enjoyed having that information."

Those words touched that raw place in Amelia's gut that still stung with humiliation.

"Those women wouldn't keep their mouths shut if their lives depended on it," Ruth said. "I know you're not like that. But I just don't have anything to say. Not now. Maybe not ever." She took a deep breath.

Amelia wondered if she should bring up the trip to Vegas.

"I'm sure you'll hear that I'm going to Vegas. Some people might think it's too soon. My husband was just buried the day before yesterday. But I'm going. I'm leaving in a few days."

"Um, the police don't mind? You're not worried about that?"

"They have the man that did it," Ruth said. "They don't need me."

"Oh, of course."

"I don't mean to be rude, Amelia. You've never been anything but nice to me, but you've got to leave now."

"Ruth, please, if you know—"

"Thanks again for the spaghetti," Ruth repeated robotically as she motioned for

Amelia to head toward the door. "Tell the kids. Thanks for stopping by."

As the door slammed, Amelia found herself outside on the porch.

She climbed into her truck and frantically fished through her purse. The overhead light was weaker than a candle. Finally, squinting and searching through receipts and junk in her purse, she found her wallet and rifled through it.

"Gotcha!" she said. It was a tiny rectangle, Detective Walishovsky's business card. He had to know that Ruth was leaving town. If that didn't scream of a guilty conscience or at least the accomplice of a guilty conscience, what did?

She sped home in time to see John's Suburban sitting in the driveway. Parking the big pink truck, she climbed out all smiles, as if nothing was wrong. The kids had their own keys. John could have let them in to wait by themselves. They weren't babies anymore.

"Hey, guys!" She waved.

Meg jumped out and ran to hug her. "Hi, Mom."

Her daughter always seemed to get a little taller every time she came back. Amelia was sure that was all in her head, but Meg was so beautiful to her it was lovely and sad to see her grow up.

"Hey, Mom." Adam waved as he sauntered to the door. Taking his key out of his pocket, he unlocked the front door, turned on the lights, and waited.

"Everything good?" Amelia asked John, who looked at her with a sour grimace.

"I said I was bringing them back at seven o'clock."

Amelia looked at her watch. It was seven-thirty on the dot.

"Sorry, John, but I got hung up at work."

"How can that be? It's a truck. You drive your job wherever you go!"

"Meg, go on in the house."

Without a word, Meg quickly ran up to her brother, who took her by the shoulder and gently led her inside.

"I'm sorry I was half an hour late for the first time in over a year since the divorce. How horrible it must have been for you to sit in the driveway with your children just a little longer than necessary." Her voice dripped venom that was bubbling over from the comments Ruth had made.

John clenched the steering wheel. "This is how it starts, Amelia—this job you've got." He waved his hand at the truck as he did the last time she'd seen him at Food Truck Alley. "It's just going to require more and more time. You're late once, then it will become habitual, then the kids will start to suffer. I've seen it a million times, Amelia. You are no exception."

"I find it really surprising how interested you are in what I do now, but when we were married..." She held her breath. Amelia knew she could go on about his affair and his poor handling of the kids, not to mention her. It was as easy as shooting fish in a barrel. But she didn't say any more. Instead, she bit her tongue. "Thanks for bringing the kids home, John, and for sitting with them. I appreciate it." She started to walk toward the front door.

"Is that it? Is that all you have to say?"

Fueled by fury, her blood raced through her veins, making Amelia clench her fists. She turned, walked up to the driver's side of his car, and leaned down at the window. "Please don't criticize the Pink Cupcake in front of the kids, especially Meg. She helped me pick out the color and the name."

It was obvious from his expression that John had been doing that but had no idea Meg was so involved in Amelia's business. He clenched his jaw but nodded. It had to have felt like an utter surrender to him. Without another word, he put the car in reverse and pulled out of the driveway.

Smiling to herself, Amelia walked in the front door.

"So, what was that all about?" Adam asked, holding an empty banana peel in one hand and an apple with a bite already taken out of it in the other.

"Where's your sister?"

"She went upstairs already." Adam crunched into his apple. "Is everything all right with Dad?"

"Oh, sure. It's fine."

"He sounded really mad."

Amelia looked at her son and saw that rebellious streak flicker in his eyes. He was ready and willing to pick a side, and Amelia was warmed by the fact that he would have been on hers. However, as she had promised herself long before, she refused to talk badly about the kids' father, no matter how much the jackass might have deserved it.

"Your father doesn't like to be kept waiting. I've known that for years. It's no big deal. He'll be back in two weeks like normal." Amelia smiled and looked at the apple core in her son's hand. "How about a bologna sandwich? I think there are chips in the cabinet."

"Okay."

"Why is your sister upstairs?" In the kitchen, Amelia prepared the sandwich on white with just a squirt of mustard, the way Adam liked it.

"Dad told her she's not allowed to work at the Cupcake."

"Why? Did he say?" She handed him the sandwich.

Adam took a big bite out of it and shrugged. "Maybe because of the murder? Maybe he thought she'd work with him, filing or something. Maybe he's just realized his mortality," he said with his mouth full.

Amelia nodded and frowned a little. "Hey, you and your sister want to watch a movie upstairs in the big bed, like you used to when you were kids?"

"Can't. I've got homework."

"You were supposed to finish that before you left with your father."

Adam shrugged and headed down the stairs to the basement/cave.

After making another sandwich, Amelia put it on a plate, added a handful of potato chips and a bottle of water from the fridge, and marched upstairs.

She knocked gently on her daughter's door and waited until she heard the quiet "come in" from Meg.

Pushing the door open with the plate, Amelia smiled at her daughter, who was lying on her bed with her headphones on. The room was a light blue that Amelia had promised to repaint in any color Meg wanted as soon as she had some time and extra money. In the meantime, there were dozens of pictures and posters of current celebrity heartthrobs on the walls. One poster had a giant brown Domo standing in the street in front of a tiny man, with the caption Don't Be Afraid to Stand Up against Your Problems. Her corkboard was covered with pictures of her and her friends from school, ticket stubs, and postcards. Her small dresser was covered with jewelry and hairspray bottles and perfume. And of course, there were clothes all over the place.

"Hey. I brought you a sandwich," Amelia said.

"Thanks, Mom. I'm not all that hungry."

"Well, keep it. Just in case you want a late-night snack while you are texting Katherine or whatever."

"Okay."

"Is everything all right?" Amelia asked.

"Adam told you, didn't he?"

"Told me what?"

"That Dad said I couldn't work at the Cupcake."

Amelia set the plate on her daughter's dresser, pushing aside a couple books she was reading and an old empty Coke can. She sat down on the bed, making it squeak. "Yeah, he told me."

"I'm sorry." Meg's eyes filled with tears. "I thought he'd be proud of me because I was showing initiative, like he always says teenagers need to do."

"Well, working a job is not something I'm ever going to say no to. If you want to work with your mom at the Cupcake, then you will. And you'll surprise the heck out of your dad when he realizes how great you'll be at it."

"What if he gets mad?"

"I'll talk to him. He won't. He might not understand that you'd never be there alone, that you won't be driving the truck and all that. You'll be helping. I need some good help. He'll be cool with it."

Meg smiled and reached for a chip from the plate. "Can I come to work with you tomorrow?"

"Tomorrow is a school day."

"So?"

"So, no," Amelia said. "You go to school."

"Fine, deprive me of real-life experiences. I may as well be raised by the television."

"Where do you and your brother come up with this stuff? You're both too deep for me." She kissed her daughter on the head and went to her own room.

Before long, she was falling asleep herself. Despite her fatigue, the information she had stumbled on that night kept rolling around in her mind.

Ruth Indesh was, for lack of a better term, skipping town. Matthew Rodriguez didn't

143

have access to a knife like the one found at the crime scene. The motive was skimpy at best. And who was that blond woman at the Gamblers Anonymous meeting who was falling to pieces at the mere mention of Peter's name? It was like a tornado of information. It was all there swirling around, but somewhere, somehow, it was all linked together.

Amelia had to find out who that blond woman was. Something in her gut told her she was the answer. But that would mean waiting a week for another Gamblers Anonymous meeting. Matthew was going to be transferred as soon as his case was brought to a preliminary hearing. She would be cutting it close, at best.

She fell into a restless sleep, and the morning would start out tumultuous as well.

Chapter Seventeen

"Amelia!" Lila was waving wildly as the Pink Cupcake pulled up and backed into its slot at Food Truck Alley. She ran around to the driver's side and knocked on the door. "You gotta let me in."

"Yes, yes. Of course." Amelia quickly shut off the engine, ran to the back, and unlocked the big door.

Within seconds, Lila was inside the truck, closing and locking the door behind her.

"What is the matter with you?"

"Okay, I just happened to get here a little sooner than usual. So I thought I'd be a good neighbor and check in on some of our food-truck friends." Lila turned on all the ovens and began folding the pink paper boats as usual while she spoke a mile a minute. "So,

I said hi to Philly Cheesesteak, and when he didn't fall down on the ground and ask me to marry him, I went over to Turkey Club and nearly got my behind handed to me." Lila jerked her thumb to the right, in the direction of the Turkey Club.

"What did you do?"

"I just walked up to the back door, knocked on the metal, and said, 'Hello, good morning.'"

Amelia waited. "And?"

"She turned to look at me, gave me a once-over, and started shouting, 'Would you get out of here! Get out of here! I'm not afraid to use this knife!'"

Amelia poured a steaming cup of hot water into a Styrofoam cup and dropped a chamomile tea bag into it. "She actually said, 'I'm not afraid to use this knife'?"

"As sure as I'm sitting here, she said it." Lila wrapped her hands around the warm Styrofoam. "And I think she's living out of that truck. There are rules against that, aren't there?"

"Why do you say that?"

"Well, there was an open suitcase in the back, a grocery bag full of tape, some filthy sheets, spray paint, cans of vegetables... Weird."

Amelia got up from her seat across the small table from Lila and went toward the door.

"What are you doing?"

"I'm not going to have anyone abusing my staff... but me," Amelia muttered. "I'll go get it straightened out. We don't want conflict when we all have to do business together, but there is no excuse for that."

"Here, just in case. Take my mace. It shoots up to twenty feet and is a bright-green dye." Lila handed Amelia a little vial of toxic chemicals.

Amelia looked at the little black sprayer and tucked it into a pocket. "I doubt it will come to that, but better safe than sorry."

She climbed out of her truck and walked toward the front window of the Turkey Club. It was open, and the delicious smell of the bird cooked every Thanksgiving filled her nose. How could you be mean when you were surrounded by that smell?

She listened and heard a woman mumbling to herself inside. Was she on the phone? Was there someone else in there? Too late to worry about that.

Amelia had not exchanged more than a wave or a nod with her food-truck neighbor to the right. But when she walked up to the window, she froze.

The blonde at the Gamblers Anonymous meeting! That was where Amelia had seen her—right next door to her own truck!

"What do you want?" The woman barked. She was a totally different woman from the sobbing, nearly hysterical creature that had acted so frail and delicate at the GA meeting.

"Hi. I own the Pink Cupcake next door."

"Yes?"

"My coworker said you had a few words with her. We certainly don't want any trouble, but can I ask if there is a problem or something?"

The woman seemed to be caught off guard. "I didn't realize she worked for you. I thought she was a transient. You just can't really tell anymore, these days."

"My name is Amelia Harley."

"Trudy Giles." She let out a loud sigh of annoyance at having to introduce herself, but she did give Amelia a wave with a long carving knife. "I'd shake your hand, but I'm covered in turkey."

"It's nice to meet you, Trudy. The woman you spoke with this morning is my employee, Lila Bergman. You'll be seeing her a lot since she's with me every day."

"Thanks for letting me know. You can never be too sure." She didn't look up as she spoke, as if she were performing a very delicate surgery, dismembering the dead bird on her counter.

"So, I'm surprised we didn't meet sooner with that murder getting all of us involved. I'm pretty spooked about it."

"I'm not. I didn't know the man." She continued to cut the meat. "Besides, they caught the animal that did it. There isn't anything left to be scared of. Unless they decide not to move this bucket of beans and bolts next to me out of here."

"You mean Mrs. Vega's truck?" Amelia's heart was racing. She just knew she was sweating as if she were in a sauna, and her cheeks burned.

"You know them?" Trudy's question was tainted with disgust. Her eyes looked Amelia up and down. It was the same look girls in high school gave each other when checking out the competition. "Well, I'm sure they're very nice."

"They are. And Ruth Indesh is very nice, too."

"Yeah, I heard she was trouble."

Amelia couldn't believe her luck. Trudy had walked right into Amelia's trap. Just a few seconds before, the woman had claimed she didn't know the murder victim.

"Well, maybe you're right." Amelia didn't want to give herself away. "Maybe they have the wrong guy, and his wife killed him. Wives kill their husbands every day. It's not unheard of."

Amelia was concerned at how many times she'd said that over the past couple days. Her husband was a two-timing so-and-so, yet she'd never once thought about killing him. Having him beaten, yes, absolutely. But not killed.

"I don't know. But that type of woman usually pushes a guy to do things. Who knows? Look, I've got three birds in the ovens that need basting and carving, so if you'll excuse me..." Without another word, Trudy Giles went back to her work, showing Amelia nothing but her back.

"Yeah, okay. Have a nice day, Trudy."

The steps back to the Pink Cupcake were ten of the longest Amelia had ever taken. She was sure that lying woman would realize her mistake and come charging out of the food truck, carving knife raised and the fires of hell in her eyes.

But nothing happened. She was safe behind the metal door when Lila spoke, causing Amelia to jump, startled out of her trance.

"So what did she say?"

Taking her seat again, Amelia felt as if the wind had been knocked out of her. Even if that woman hadn't killed Peter, she was lying about something. With careful, quiet words, Amelia relayed exactly what Trudy had said.

"Transient?" Lila asked. "Sorry, but I shop at only the most upscale thrift stores."

"I need to make a phone call."

Digging through her purse as if gold was at the bottom, Amelia was nearly frantic. Weird giggles came out of her throat, sounding odd and scared. "Where are you?" she muttered.

"What?" Lila asked. "You have a gun in there?"

"I wish. No. Ah ha! There you are, you little devil." She pulled out a business card and showed Lila.

"Detective Walishovsky." Lila looked at the front and back of the card. "Well, if nothing else, he'll be happy to hear from you."

"Can you be serious? We have the real killer next to us. I'm sure of it. And you want to focus on my love life?"

"I don't want to focus on it. I'm just saying. Okay, call that number and get some squads and some men in uniform and SWAT if necessary to wrangle this harlot out of here."

"Wrangle? Harlot? Where do you come from?"

Lila smiled. "I can't help it. I talk like old westerns sometimes when I get nervous."

Amelia shook her head and dialed the detective's number.

Holding the phone to her ear, she looked at Lila. "I'm nervous," she said with one hand over the mouthpiece.

"Me too," Lila whispered.

"Walishovsky," the detective barked into the phone.

"Oh, uh, hi, Detective. This is Amelia Harley. I was with you yesterday. I mean, not with you—I saw you at the station yesterday. I had come to see Matthew Rodriguez for a few minutes. It was just a brief amount of time. I don't know if you remember."

"I remember you, Miss Harley. What can I do for you?"

"Well, I'm not quite sure how to say this, but you've got the wrong guy."

"You said that yesterday, Miss Harley. I'll need a little more than your strong conviction."

"I've got proof." She let out a deep breath. "Well, maybe not proof, but I've certainly found a person of interest. No. She's more than that. I'd call her a suspect if I had to, definitely a much more serious suspect than Matthew Rodriguez."

"And who is this suspect you've discovered all on your own?"

Amelia didn't like his condescending tone but shook it off, realizing that in his place, she would have been skeptical, too. How many phone calls had he gotten in addition to hers that were total crackpots looking for publicity?

"I don't want to discuss this over the phone. Can you come to Food Truck Alley?"

"Miss Harley, this is unusual, to say the least."

"It's a tip, isn't it? A lead? You have to check it out. That's in the policeman's code or something."

"Yeah, the policeman's code. Okay, Miss Harley. I'll be there in about half an hour."

"Okay, but don't come like a detective. Just come by like you want a cupcake and just happen to be in the neighborhood. But stay away from the Turkey Club."

"What?"

"The food truck to my left," she said. "I'm the Pink Cupcake. You can't miss my truck."

"I remember what it looks like. That's a color you can't forget."

"My daughter picked it out. I'll tell her you like it. Just please get here. Thank you, Detective."

Amelia hung up. She looked at Lila, and they made the cupcakes. Both women were silent, as if listening for any sign of trouble.

Trouble sometimes comes as a whisper.

Chapter Eighteen

Half an hour passed with no sign of Detective Walishovsky. Then an hour passed. Then two hours. The lunchtime rush washed over the Pink Cupcake and all the other trucks. Amelia and Lila became so busy they almost forgot they'd been waiting for the detective. When things finally settled, Lila grabbed a bottle of water, and Amelia began cleaning up.

"You don't think he ditched us, do you?" Lila tilted the bottle way back and took a big gulp.

"He can't. If a policeman ignores a tip, and it turns out to be valuable, he could get in trouble. I don't take Detective Walishovsky as the kind of guy to go against protocol. Do you?" Amelia shook her head as she spoke and swept up the flour on her worktable, scratching her nose in the process and turning it completely white with powder.

"No, I don't. I also don't think he'd pass up the opportunity to come talk to you." Lila set down her water and got to work on the receipts.

"I don't know where you get that idea from."

"A woman knows."

"Yeah." Amelia started to protest but stopped midsentence. Her eyes had just happened to fall on the mirror outside the back of her truck. It was a small circular mirror that gave a view of the blind side of the truck in case the staff was going in and out through the back door. It was especially valuable if a food truck did catering. Carrying out delicacies in a timely fashion depended on few accidents and spills while moving them from the truck to an event.

"What is it?" Lila looked toward the open door at the back of the truck.

"My mirror." Amelia pointed.

Lila looked and gasped. "What is that?"

Amelia got up and walked over to the mirror. "What color was that spray-paint you saw in the truck next door?"

Swallowing hard, Lila nodded her head "It had a black cap on it. I assume it was black."

The mirror had been sprayed black. Nothing could be seen in it. Amelia became angry. Those little mirrors cost twenty dollars at most, and Adam could surely figure out how to remove the old one and attach a new one, but as Amelia looked up at it, she felt a familiar sting in her eyes.

"Are you all right, Amelia?" Lila asked.

"Lila, my ex-husband thinks this truck is an embarrassment. He thinks my business is a joke and reflects badly on him. He left me for a woman only twenty-five years old." Tears fell from the corners of her eyes.

Lila nodded, gave her all her attention, and didn't speak.

"He left me with two teenagers to raise without a job and an alimony payment that is so small only the government pays out less to people."

Lila chuckled but still remained silent.

Pointing at the mirror with her fingers digging into her palm, Amelia shook her head. "This truck was my kids' idea." She wrapped her arms tightly around her own waist. "They love my baking. They said I was better at it than any of the other moms at their school. They helped me through the entire process of filling out the paperwork to buying this beast to getting the menu down pat to picking the name and the color. To insult the Pink Cupcake is like insulting my kids. And I won't stand for it. Not from John. Not from anyone."

She inhaled deeply and let her breath out slowly as Lila stood and wrapped Amelia in her arms with a tender squeeze.

"What should we do?" Lila asked.

"I'll tell you what I'm going to do. I'm going to confront Miss Giles." Amelia hopped down off the back of the truck before Lila had a chance to talk her out of it and convince her to wait for Detective Walishovsky.

Banging loudly on the open back door of the Turkey Club, Amelia expected to catch Trudy off guard. She couldn't have been more wrong.

"You again?" Trudy asked in a huffy voice.

"Why did you spray-paint my mirror?"

"Spray-paint your what?"

Amelia reached into the back, next to the open door, and pulled out the can of black spray paint.

"My mirror. Did you do this today while we were busy? Maybe yesterday?"

"Shows how much you care about your truck. I did it after you followed me to the Gamblers Anonymous meeting." She glared at Amelia. "How many days ago was that?"

"Gamblers Anonymous? What are you talking about?" Amelia asked.

"I saw you loitering in the rain, spying on me. You're a terrible detective and should leave it to the professionals. Well, they are pretty incompetent, too."

"You did it. You killed Peter Indesh. I know you did."

"Really? And how are you going to prove that, little miss investigator? You're divorced. You are struggling to feel needed, wanted. No one is going to believe you."

"I don't need to prove it. The police will. They are on their way over here because I called them. I told them how you lied about knowing Peter, how you insinuated his wife had something to do with it."

"She did!" Trudy yelled. "She practically pushed him onto the knife." Her voice became a menacing hiss. "She gambled all their money away. Peter was doing everything he could to keep a roof over their head. He went without everything. And what did she do? Just took his paycheck to the liquor store, cashed it, and gave the money to the cashier for twenty or thirty scratch-offs before she went back home. She'd have her unemployment directly deposited, and that money would go into her online gambling account."

"And what? You thought you could help him?"

"He wouldn't leave her. He just wouldn't."

"So you move on, Trudy. You don't kill a man and then let an innocent man take the blame! How crazy are you?"

"That was the beauty of it. I hated having those people working next to me. Hearing their obnoxious music and watching that old woman in the black doting on that big, fat dummy of a son. And now they are gone, too."

"That was Mrs. Vega's nephew," Amelia spat. "And you are worse than I can even imagine. I might be able to understand a broken heart, but your heart isn't broken. It's diseased. And I'm getting the cops here right now."

Amelia turned to leave and climb back into the Pink Cupcake, but Trudy was in front of her before she could take half a step. The large carving knife was in her right hand, held close to her chest while her back was to the ever-dwindling crowd of people.

"Get in the truck," she hissed, her left hand clamping down on Amelia's arm.

Chapter Nineteen

Without thinking, Amelia reached for the mace Lila had given her and sprayed the neon-green pepper spray into Trudy's face.

Trudy let out a horrific scream that brought half a dozen people running in their direction, including Detective Walishovsky, his partner, and four uniformed police officers.

"Police! Get your hands where I can see them!" Detective Walishovsky yelled.

Amelia dropped the mace and put her hands high in the air. Her eyes went wide, and she didn't know what to do except stand there statue still. Lila came out of the truck but also grew roots in the ground and didn't dare move as the police descended on the scene.

"Trudy Giles! You're under arrest for the murder of Maximillian Fagen," barked Eugene Gus, Detective Walishovsky's partner. He continued reading her the Miranda Rights as Trudy's eyes struggled to gape open.

She gagged and writhed on the ground while an EMT unit, that had been standing by, administered first aid to remove the toxin from her eyes.

Amelia watched the whole event unfold, unaware she was still holding her hands in the air.

"Miss Harley." Detective Walishovsky walked slowly up to her.

She stared at him, waiting for the same speech: *"You are under arrest for macing Trudy Giles. You have the right to remain silent..."*

But he didn't.

"Miss Harley. You can put your arms down now."

Amelia shook her head, feeling her cheeks flush, and quickly pulled her arms down.

"You guys got here just in time." Amelia breathed the words as if she had just run a marathon. "What was that all about? Who is Maximillian Fagen?"

"That is Trudy's common-law husband. Seems Miss Giles had been on the run for a couple of years. These food trucks are low profile, and a lot of them are seasonal. You can easily blend into the background in one of these. Unless it's a hot-pink truck with a giant cupcake on the side."

"What happened?"

"Maximillian Fagen was murdered two years ago. Stabbed over thirty times and left in a nature preserve. Long brown hair strands were found on the body. Trudy Giles, the brunette, was nowhere to be found."

"So, how come you arrested her now? How come all this time, Matthew Rodriguez has been locked up? Didn't anyone interview Trudy before?"

"Yes. My men followed protocol. But when the knife was discovered and the argument between Mr. Rodriguez and the deceased was reported by several witnesses and Mr. Rodriguez's history came to light, he was as viable a suspect as anyone else."

"But you are arresting her for killing Mr. Fagen. What about Mr. Indesh?"

"We are pretty confident that, after a thorough search of her truck, her car, and her home, we'll come up with everything we need. The pattern was the same. The weapon was the same. The thing they both have in common is Miss Giles."

"Sir?" a young uniformed officer called to the detective. "I think you better see this."

The detective excused himself and walked over to the back door of the Turkey Club. Quietly, Amelia tiptoed along behind him. The police officer, wearing thin latex gloves, was holding up a white sheet that looked as if a turkey had been shot on it. There was also half a palm print in blood, which was much larger than Trudy Giles's petite hands.

"Oh, gosh." Amelia said, putting her hand to her mouth in shock. The funny thing was that the first thing to come to her mind was how excited her kids were going to be to hear the gory details of the day's events.

"Send it to the lab" was all Detective Walishovsky said. He turned around and looked down at Amelia. "Thank you for your persistence, Miss Harley. You may have helped save the Gary Police Department from a terrible embarrassment. Of course, you won't get any credit for it, I'm afraid.

Except maybe the gratitude of a seasoned detective."

Amelia laughed out loud. "She vandalized my truck." Amelia pointed at the blackened mirror. "I think she was planning on ambushing me."

"I'll look into that for you, too. I'd hate for your kids to see it." He looked down at Amelia. His face hadn't changed—he didn't smile or grin or grimace or even tilt his head—but there was a change in his eyes. They were soft, kind, and even beautiful. Amelia smiled up at him.

"Detective? We need you in here."

With a nod of his head, Detective Walishovsky left Amelia and headed into the Turkey Club truck. Amelia would have liked to climb in too and peer around at the evidence or blood spatter or whatever it was the police were going to find. Instead, she walked to where Lila was still standing.

"What a day," Lila said. "I'm sorry. I'd move, but I think I pooped my pants."

Amelia laughed out loud. "You did not. You're fine. Come on. Let's get today wrapped up and never speak of it again." She pushed past Lila, squeezing her hand affectionately.

Following her into the back of the truck and taking her usual seat, Lila shook her head. "Amelia, I have to tell you that at all the jobs I've had, I've never had one where I felt my life was in danger. This is not normal."

Swallowing hard, Amelia turned and looked at Lila. *She's going to quit. Who in their right mind would want to work here now? Lila is right. Maybe this truck is cursed.*

"Oh, well. I understand. Asking for fifteen minutes of overtime is one thing. Asking you to witness a murderer being apprehended just ten feet away after you've worked next to that person for a few weeks, well, that's different. Um, if you can let me figure out your last check and also that finder's fee for the PB&J cupcakes, I'll—"

"Amelia, this is the best job I've ever had! You can't write this kind of stuff! You'll have to fire me before I quit this gig! And even then, I may not leave!"

"Thank goodness!" Amelia sighed and fell into her own chair. "Don't scare me like that. I've had enough scares today. Oh, here's your mace." She tossed the black sprayer to Lila.

"Was that lucky or what?"

"That was buy-a-lottery-ticket kind of lucky." Amelia's eyes widened.

"Are you sure you want to gamble on anything today or any other day?"

"Right?"

The two women talked as though they had been friends for years as they cleaned the truck and added the receipts. It was another day in the black.

Lila walked home as usual. Amelia swung by the bank as she did every night then pulled up in the driveway to both her kids bounding out of the house excitedly.

"Mom! Mom! Guess what?" Meg said.

"What? What is all the commotion?"

"Mrs. Vega and her daughter just stopped by! They brought us burritos, Spanish rice, and churros!"

"Yeah," Adam said. "You don't have to cook, Mom."

"They said Matthew was getting out of jail," Meg said. "They would be releasing him tomorrow, but they were going to go and wait for him."

"Well, isn't that good news for the Vegas." Amelia smiled. Had she seen Mrs. Vega, she probably would have started crying, and that was against the rules.

"Did you have something to do with that, Mom? Did you solve the murder?" Meg bounced up and down. Amelia could tell she was hoping for some bragging rights.

"Oh no, honey. Detective Walishovsky did. I just told him some of the stuff I was, you know, thinking about. He's a really smart guy. He figured it all out. And he said he loves our truck. Isn't that nice?"

"Come on, Mom. The food's getting cold," Adam said, pulling her by her hand into the house.

They all sat down at the kitchen table. The whole house smelled like a Mexican restaurant. The food was delicious, and the conversation was lively as Amelia told her children how the detective had caught Trudy Giles. But she left out the part about the mirror and the confrontation she'd had with Trudy.

"We should make some cupcakes for the police," Meg said.

"That is a great idea. Let's do that." Amelia rubbed her daughter's head. "How about it, Adam? Want to help?"

"If I can lick the bowl."

"No. I get to lick the bowl," Meg said.

"I think Mom gets to lick the bowl," Amelia said.

Chapter Twenty

Three days had gone by since Trudy Giles was arrested for the murder of a man by the name of Maximillian Fagen. Her truck had been confiscated and impounded, leaving a large space, like a missing tooth in the mouth of an eight-year-old.

The news had wasted no time describing in great detail the murder of Mr. Fagen and how now, three years after that case had gone cold, the murder of Peter Indesh revived it, bringing closure to both the Fagen and Indesh families.

Although Peter Indesh's body held very little evidence to go on and the knife found in the Vegas' food truck held only the victim's DNA, Trudy Giles's food truck was rife with damning evidence.

The blood spattering the sheet Lila had spotted proved to be not only Peter's blood but that of a couple turkeys as well. There was another knife found with her blood and Peter's caked on it. There was also a suicide note inside a green lockbox that held receipts. In it, Trudy had addressed Peter, stating she would end her life in front of him, in front of his wife, on their front porch if he didn't agree to see her.

The letter had never been sent. Trudy had lost control before giving Peter that morbid ultimatum.

She had developed feelings for Peter when she had met him at Gamblers Anonymous. Ruth did have a severe gambling problem. She had gotten so hooked that their home was about to be foreclosed on. Peter had drained his 401K and every credit card he had. After filing for bankruptcy a year earlier, he thought they could start over fresh, but Ruth didn't stop. Their credit was ruined, and she blamed him for not making enough money.

He started attending the GA meetings. Trudy quickly took notice of him. They talked more and more frequently. Sharing intimate details about their lives and feelings and hopes, Trudy began to assume the role of girlfriend.

There was no evidence that they had ever been intimate—no motel receipts or trysts at her apartment—but Peter had been spotted at her truck quite a few times.

They would have deep conversations, and Trudy was always touching his hands or giving him long, tight hugs before he left.

But when Peter decided to stand by Ruth, to help her with her addiction and rebuild their marriage, Trudy became furious. He had tried several times to explain to her that he loved his wife despite her short-comings. Trudy was having none of that. In her mind, she and Peter had already been more intimate with each other than mere flesh could achieve. Their souls were joined.

As with most crimes of passion, Trudy believed if she couldn't have Peter, then no one should.

She confessed to killing him and Maximillian Fagen before they had even taken her mug shot and fingerprints.

Chapter Twenty-One

When Amelia pulled into her slot at Food Truck Alley that day, she was happy to see Mrs. Vega back at her truck, wearing her same black dress and Nikes, scribbling the day's specials on her board.

After putting the truck in park and shutting off the engine, Amelia, having invested in a magnetic board with letters, went around the front of the truck to list the day's specials: apple-crisp cupcakes, double chocolate-fudge cupcakes, and the new item, a bacon-and-cheddar cupcake that was more like a biscuit than a cupcake.

When she turned around, she saw the smiling face of Matthew Rodriguez. He was holding a gift.

"Hi, Matthew," she said. "What is this?"

"Just a little something I picked up for you. To say thank you."

"Matthew, you and your aunt have fed me and my entire family for the past two days. You don't owe me anything."

"Miss Harley, if it weren't for you, I would still be in that jail. They'd be getting ready to move me to the courthouse prison. My aunt would never be able to get there every day and back again. Miss Harley, I owe you everything." He handed her a brown box.

Without saying anything, Amelia opened it and pulled out an item from the bubble wrap. As she gently unwrapped it, she smiled wildly. It was a new mirror for the rear of her truck in the shape of a diamond and painted hot pink.

"Matthew, it's beautiful!" She stood on tiptoe and hugged the big brute.

He stooped and gently patted her back as if patting too hard could cause damage to a delicate female. "I'll put it on for you."

"That would be great."

Mrs. Vega came over, her eyes red with tears of joy, and hugged Amelia tightly.

"How's business, Mrs. Vega?" Amelia asked. "Does it feel good to be back?"

"We're blessed, Miss Harley. With friends like you, I never have to worry about my beautiful nephew. Do you see his gift? His cousin's boyfriend made that custom. He has a shop in town."

"It's wonderful. I really appreciate it."

"Well, it's the least we could do since that devil ruined yours."

Mrs. Vega didn't mince words when it came to Trudy Giles. Even though she was a devout Catholic, she cursed the woman's name in English and in Spanish.

Not five minutes later, Matthew had installed the new mirror, and it was a perfect match. Amelia decided it was her favorite part of the truck.

After a few more hugs and kind words, Mrs. Vega and Matthew went back to the Burrito Wagon to get ready for the morning rush, and Amelia finished listing her specials.

Lila saw the mirror right away. "That looks great!" she said, climbing into the back of the truck. "When did you get that replaced?"

"Matthew had it made for us."

"That guy is a giant creampuff. What a sweetheart."

"I know." Amelia said as she distributed the morning ingredients between the two of them.

"Now, are you ready for some more good news?" Lila asked.

"I don't know if I can take it. I'm smiling so much people are starting to think I am insane."

"Well, I got a call from Darcy last night."

"Who?"

"Darcy?"

Amelia shook her head.

"Darcy? The officer at the front desk who got you in to see Matthew when he was locked up?"

"Oh, yeah, your new best buddy. Yes, I remember Darcy."

"Well, you remember she is getting married," Lila said. "After you and the kids dropped off those cupcakes at the precinct, she went nuts for them. She wants to know if you'll cater her wedding shower and provide cupcakes for the wedding."

"Really?"

Lila nodded and smiled. "Please don't tell me you don't think you're up to it. You've been managing this truck like you're born to do it. Your books prove people like your product. Just start small by offering a couple of options, like three or four that they can pick from, and whip them up." Lila counted on her bright-red manicured fingers. "It's no different than what you do here every day except you know exactly how many to make, what kind, and by when. Yikes, Amelia! It sounds even easier than doing this every day!"

Holding her breath and thinking of the possibilities, Amelia nodded yes.

"Fantastic! I told her you'd meet with her on Saturday morning with your four most popular cupcakes, enough for her and her mother and three sisters to sample for the shower."

"What?" Amelia gasped. "What if I would have said no?"

"I haven't known you as long as some people have, Amelia. But I know one thing for sure, and that is you aren't afraid to try."

"Knock knock!" said a familiar voice outside the truck. Amelia turned around to see Christine waving wildly.

"Hey, girl!" Amelia squealed. "What are you doing here?"

"I'm ashamed it's taken me so long to come by. This truck looks a-mazing!"

"Well, hold on and let me get you something. Christine, this is my good friend and business advisor, Lila Bergman. Lila, this is Christine Mills. If you ever need to know where the bodies are buried, Christine can tell you."

The ladies laughed as Amelia poured three Styrofoam cups of hot water and dropped an Earl Grey teabag in each.

For a few minutes, they talked until Christine finally asked about the arrest of Trudy Giles.

"The police can't say anything," Lila said, "but your friend here played a very big part in getting that trash picked up."

"I knew it," Christine said. "As soon as I heard the news, I knew you had a hand in that. Good for you, Amelia."

"I'm just hoping that if I ever get accused of murder, someone will do the same for me."

"Speaking of committing murder, have you heard from John lately?" Christine asked, making Lila chuckle.

"Uh, no. No, I haven't heard a word from him. He's got the kids this weekend, and, well, seems I have a catering job to solidify." Amelia nudged Lila.

"Catering? That's great!"

The women chatted for a few more moments before Christine looked at her watch and told them she had to leave for a dentist appointment just two blocks away.

"Stop back on your way home and I'll have a double chocolate-fudge cupcake with your name on it waiting for you," Amelia said.

"After the dentist? Perfect!" Christine shook Lila's hand and gave Amelia a good-bye hug, promising to see them both after her appointment.

The morning rush was hectic as always. The truck was hot after two rounds of cupcakes had been pulled out of them and new batches put in, with timers set for fifteen minutes each.

The guy from the Philly Cheesesteak truck leaned out the window and waved when things settled down a little. Lila waved back, and Amelia gave a quick salute before looking away and focusing on the frosting petals she was making.

"Why don't you bring him a cupcake?" Lila said.

"He's not my type."

"What? So single, muscular, gray around the temples, and piercing blue eyes isn't your type?" Lila folded her arms.

"No. Not really."

"Well, please tell me what is your type so I don't waste my time trying to make you happy."

Just then, Amelia's phone went off in her pocket. She looked at the phone number, swallowed hard, and pushed the green button that said Answer Call.

She turned away from Lila and lowered her voice. "This is Amelia."

On the other end, a man cleared his throat. "Miss Harley, this is Detective Walishovsky."

"Hello, Detective. How are you?"

"I'm doing well. How are things at the Pink Cupcake?"

"Business is good. Thanks for asking. What can I do for you?" Amelia looked at herself in the glass of the top oven and straightened her hair.

"Well, I just wanted to say thank you for the delicious cupcakes you sent over to the precinct. The officers really appreciated it. It keeps morale up when someone from the public sector does something like that. So, on behalf of the FOP of Gary, I just wanted to say thanks."

"My gosh, Detective. I should be thanking you."

"For what?"

"Well, for believing me enough to look into Trudy Giles's background and get Matthew Rodriguez out of that jail."

"We aren't in the business of prosecuting innocent people. But you see how well the machine works when the police and the public are on the same page?"

Amelia smiled. "I'd say so."

"You know, Miss Harley, I'm sorry that you didn't get any credit in the papers for your contribution to bringing Miss Giles to justice. But if you are ever in need of any assistance, day or night, rain or shine, I would consider it an honor and a privilege if you'd call on me."

Amelia swallowed hard. Suddenly, her mouth was dry, and she felt her cheeks heat up as if someone had opened one of her ovens. "That is very kind of you, Detective. I will do that. Thank you."

The line was quiet for a few seconds. Amelia cleared her throat, as did the detective.

Finally, he spoke. "Well, I've got a mountain of paperwork. Have a good day, Miss Harley."

"You do the same, Detective."

She pulled the phone away from her ear, looked at the number, and saved it in her contact list. Taking a deep breath, she looked up to see Lila, her arms folded across her chest, her chin lifted, while her eyes were devious little slits.

"Detective Walishovsky?" Lila asked.

"He was just calling to say thanks for the cupcakes."

"If you say so. But from the color of your cheeks, I think his message was a lot more than that."

Amelia shook her head and smiled. Without another word, they worked to clean up from the morning rush and prepare for noon. People would be longing for their afternoon sugar rushes and making beelines to the hot-pink truck.

At three thirty, two more familiar faces stopped by.

"Hey, kids!" Amelia leaned out the truck window to give Meg and Adam kisses on their heads. She introduced them to Lila and handed each one an apple-crisp cupcake for the journey home.

"Mom, the Cupcake was on the news again. That Trudy lady was sentenced. Everyone in school saw it on Channel One News," Meg boasted.

"Oh, my." Amelia wondered how long it would take before John saw that and had another one of his fits.

"Some kids think it's morbid. But my friends think it's cool," Adam said, jerking his dark hair to the side, away from his eyes.

A familiar buzz went off in Amelia's pocket. Pulling it out, she looked at the number. It was John.

She looked at her children, who were smiling and laughing as they told Lila about their day at school. She hit the red Decline button and joined in their conversation. They'd only be this age for a little while longer. Amelia didn't want to miss any of it.

Recipe 1: Raspberry Chocolate Cupcakes

Ingredients:

- 1 1/2 cups all-purpose flour
- 1/2 cup granulated sugar
- 1/2 cup brown sugar
- 3/4 tsp. baking soda
- 4 tbsp. butter, cubed
- 2 oz. semi-sweet baking chocolate, chopped
- 1/4 cup cocoa powder
- 1/2 cup boiling water
- 1/2 cup buttermilk
- 1/3 cup sour cream
- 2 large eggs
- 1/4 tsp. salt

Frosting:

- 1/2 cup fresh raspberries
- 1/2 cup butter
- 4 oz. cream cheese
- 3 1/2 to 4 cups powdered sugar
- 1/4 tsp. vanilla

Preheat oven to 350°F. Mix flour, sugar, salt and baking soda in a bowl. Put the butter, chocolate, and cocoa in another bowl and pour in boiling water. Cover with plastic wrap and let sit for 2 minutes. Mix until smooth. Add in buttermilk, sour cream, and eggs. Whisk until smooth.

Line a muffin tin with 15 cupcake liners. Pour 1/4 cup batter into each liner. Bake for 15 to 20 minutes, until toothpick comes out clean. Let cupcakes cool in tin for 5 minutes before moving them to cooling racks.

For frosting: Puree raspberries in a food processor or blender. Optional: press puree through strainer to get rid of the seeds.

Beat butter and cream cheese until smooth. Add powdered sugar while beating for 2 to 3 minutes. Add raspberry puree and vanilla. Beat until combined. Pipe frosting onto the cupcakes using a pastry bag fitted with a piping tip.

Recipe 2: Lemon Poppyseed Cupcakes

Ingredients:
- ½ cup butter
- 2 eggs
- 1 3/4 cups all-purpose flour
- 2 tsp. poppy seeds
- 1 1/2 tsp. baking powder
- 1/2 tsp. salt
- 1 1/2 tsp. lemon extract
- 1 cup sugar
- 1/2 tsp. vanilla
- 2/3 cup milk
- 2 tsp shredded lemon peel
- 3 tbsp. lemon juice

Lemon Glaze:

- 1 cup sugar
- 5 tsp. lemon juice
- 1/2 tsp. lemon peel

Preheat oven to 350°F. Let butter and eggs stand at room temperature for 30 minutes. Combine flour, poppy seeds, baking powder, and salt.

In another bowl, beat butter on medium-to-high speed. Add lemon extract, sugar, and vanilla. Beat for 2 minutes more or until light and fluffy. Add eggs, one at a time, while beating well. Add flour mixture and milk, beating on low speed until well combined. Stir in lemon peel and lemon juice.

Line muffin tins. Fill each 3/4 full. Bake for 10 to 12 minutes or until toothpick comes out clean. Let cupcakes cool in tin for 5 minutes before moving them to cooling racks.

For lemon glaze, combine sugar and lemon juice. Stir in lemon peel.

Spread lemon glaze on cupcakes. Let stand for 10 minutes.

Sweets and a Stabbing

About the Author

Harper Lin is the USA TODAY bestselling author of *The Patisserie Mysteries*, *The Emma Wild Holiday Mysteries*, *The Wonder Cats Mysteries*, and *The Cape Bay Cafe Mysteries*.

When she's not reading or writing mysteries, she loves going to yoga classes, hiking, and hanging out with her family and friends.

www.HarperLin.com

Sweets and a Stabbing